CROSS CHECK!

CROSS CHECK!

__Barney Holden__ & and the Birth of
Professional Hockey in North America

Daniel T. Holden

Edited by Sandra Holden Price-Hosie

Published by Aventine Press
1745 La Maderia Dr SW
Palm Bay, FL 32908
www.aventinepress.com

ISBN: 1-59330-211-8

This book would not be possible if not for the help and support of the following individuals:

Barbara, Rachel, and Kathleen Holden, for their ongoing love, guidance, and support…and for allowing Dad to monopolize the family P.C.; Charlotte Dossett Holden, and Danny Holden, Sr., for their gift of narration and articulation; Sandra Holden Price-Hosie, Susan Holden Irving, Eddie Holden, and Terry Holden, for helping to recall days-gone-by with Barney and the Holden clan in Vancouver, B.C., Canada; Mary Wilkinson Holden, for taking the time to lovingly assemble Barney's hockey scrapbook. "Professor" Harold C. Dorn, Oregon State University, the coolest "prof" ever. William Sproule, Civil & Environmental Engineering, Michigan Technological University, who gave me lots of "good stuff!" Ernie Fitzsimmons, for all of the photos, great information, and for writing the forward to this book; Lee Murray, for help and support; legendsofhockey. net, Society of International Hockey Research (SIHR); Ed Sweeney, Manitoba Hockey Hall of Fame, Inc.; James Milks, Losthockey.com, for data and statistics; Tom King, "The Hockey King," for providing more data and statistics; Connie Julian, Copper County Hockey Historian, who has been busy planning the 100th anniversary celebration of professional hockey in Houghton, Michigan in September 2004; Eric Whitehead, for his book on Fred "Cyclone" Taylor, Barney's teammate and friend; Daniel S. Mason, Faculty of Physical Education and Recreation, University of Alberta, for his extensive research on the International Hockey League; Ray Nelson, Flying Rhinoceros, Inc, for help with the cover design, photos, and valuable advice.

FOREWORD

by **Ernie Fitzsimmons**
President
Society for International Hockey Research

In my nearly forty years of researching hockey history, I have come to the conclusion that the most interesting era of hockey, by far, is the 1900's.

Prior to the turn of the Twentieth Century, hockey was mostly an enjoyable game played by those with higher incomes in the larger communities. The 1900's brought about a time where entrepreneurs began stacking teams in an attempt to win various trophies, including the Stanley Cup. Players were enticed to move from one community to another to play this exciting game.

There were no organizations controlling all of hockey, as would occur later, and many parts of Western Canada were just beginning to expand their population enough to be able to field good hockey teams. Players were free to drift from one town to another, sometimes during the same season, wherever they received the best financial offer.

Hockey equipment was now being mass produced so that most people could afford at least the bare essentials, like skates, since little equipment was worn in those days.

Newspapers finally started dedicating an entire page to sports. Hockey games were now looked forward to eagerly, and early forms of hockey advertising started to appear as well.

It is against this backdrop that the story of Barney Holden unfolds. Here is a player who was probably content playing in the city league in Winnipeg, until someone got the bright idea that he was pretty good .

He was soon playing with Hall-of-Famers like Cyclone Taylor, Newsy Lalonde, Didier Pitre and others, and he never took a backward step.

Although not considered a Hall-of-Famer, every team always craved a tough hombre like Barney. His story is an important glimpse at the pioneer era of professional hockey.

"These fellows have invented a game that is played on ice. They havefashioned knives which are fastened on their boots, and they skate ateach other in a menacing manner as they pursue a black rubber disk and propel it towards their opponent's wicket. There is great noise and threatening as they advance toward the goal, brandishing their dangerous weapons at the enemy."

> *- Description by an Englishman in the late 1800's*
> *on the newly invented game of ice hockey.*

"I once went to a fight the other night and a hockey game broke out."

> *- Rodney Dangerfield*

"A gentleman?! Ha! He was one of the dirtiest players out there!"

> *- Mary Wilkinson Holden, when asked to confirm that her husband,*
> *"Barney" Holden, was a true gentleman hockey player*

To my old softball teammates, the "Caboosemen" of Tualatin Hills. Despite the fact that you were all basically nuts, we still managed to win a league championship or two.

And to my new teammates, the Oregon Rugby Sports Union "Jesters." Thanks for letting the "old boy" come out and play one last time.

INTRODUCTION

Long before there was an Eddie Shore, or a Bobby Hull, or a Wayne Gretzky, or even (God help us) the Hanson Brothers of *Slap Shot* fame, there were the Victorian era hockey pioneers, from the Canadian provinces.

They played with little or no protective equipment and subsequently had little or no front teeth. They played for the love of the game; not in the big Canadian cities, but in the turn-of-the century mining towns of Rat Portage, Haileybury, Cobalt, and Houghton. They played at a time when substitutions were not allowed, and the only way to leave the ice was to be carried off. As a result, the opposition sought out the best players from the other team for a quick extermination. That was the origin of *goon* hockey. Surprisingly, a number of these players survived to play for a decade, or even two, as leagues in Canada and the United States formed, failed, re-formed, and finally metamorphosed into the National Hockey League. But little has been written about these old-timers. A few of the ancient superstars have popped up in a handful of hockey books, but the ink devoted to these guys is pretty sparse. But almost nothing has been written about the other fellows who paved the way and helped make the game what it is today. So as a result, I chose to write about this particular period in sports history by focusing on my grandfather, Bernard "Barney" Holden - a guy who had his bell rung more times than a San Francisco trolley. Not only was he one of the very first professional hockey players in history, but he scored the first goal, in the first game, of the very first professional hockey league game on December 9, 1904 in the Pittsburgh Duquesne Gardens. While he was certainly a star in his day, he wasn't a super-star, and you won't find him in the Hockey Hall-of-Fame. He was a defenseman…a hitter, and one rough, tough son-of-a-gun who gave as good as he got. And somewhere on the ice rinks between Michigan, Manitoba, Quebec, and Saskatchewan, he left his blood and most of his front teeth.

In compiling the record of Barney's career, I relied on the newspaper clippings from his now 100 year old scrapbook, on family stories passed along to me by my father, uncle, and cousins, as well as statistics, blurbs, tidbits, anecdotes, and hard data shared with me by a number of very helpful and enthusiastic hockey historians in the U.S. and Canada.

I have tried to present the reader with a glimpse of hockey life during the Victorian era, when the British Union Jack still flew over the Canadian provinces, and of the young men who became the first hockey stars in North America. As a Winnipeg Tribune reporter reflected many years later, having grown up watching Barney and others who played on the very first professional teams, *"Those were truly the days of **He-Man** hockey!"*

DAN HOLDEN

"Hockey is a game for men;
essentially, it is a game for the youth.
It needs strong, full-blooded men.
Weaklings cannot survive in it,
the puny cannot play it,
and the timid have no place in it…"

Arthur Farrell, Hall of Fame player and early hockey author, 1910.

BERNARD "BARNEY" HOLDEN

Defense – **Cover Point, Rover**
6', 200 lbs
Born: March 21, 1881 - **Winnipeg, Manitoba**
Racial Origin – **Irish**
Religion – **Roman Catholic**
Citizenship - **Canadian**

AMATEUR

1897-98	**St. Mary's Septette** (exact yrs unk)	
1898-99	**Winnipeg Telegram** (League Champions)	
1899-02	**Canadian Pacific Railroad** (exact yrs unk)	
1902-03	**Winnipeg Shamrocks (1)**	Man. NW
1903-04	**Winnipeg Shamrocks (?)**	Man. NW

PROFESSIONAL

1904-05	**Portage Lakes** (Houghton, MI)**(2)(a)**	IHL
1905-06	**Portage Lakes** (Houghton, MI)**(b)**	IHL
1906-07	**Winnipeg Strathconas**	ManPro
	Portage Lakes (Houghton, MI)**(c)**	IHL
1907-08	**Winnipeg Maple Leafs***	ManPro
	(League Champions)	
	Winnipeg Maple Leafs	ManPro
	(Stanley Cup Contender)	
	Montreal Wanderers (3)	NHA
1908-09	**Winnipeg Maple Leafs**	ManPro
1909-10	**Montreal Shamrocks**	CHA
	Montreal Shamrocks	NHA **(4)**
	Montreal ACB	Sr. MMHL
1910-11	**Quebec Bulldogs**	NHA **(4)**
1911-12	**Saskatoon Wholesalers**	Sask-Pro
	(League Champions)	
	Saskatoon Wholesalers	Sask-Pro
	(Stanley Cup Contender)	
1912-13	**Winnipeg Victorias? (5)**	

1913-14	**Winnipeg Victorias? (5)**	?
1914-15	**Saskatoon**	Sr. XG
	(Amateur Exhibition)	

League Abbreviations:
Man NW: Manitoba Northwest Hockey Association
IHL: International Professional Hockey League
ManPro: Manitoba Pro. Hockey League (also known as MPHL)
NHA: National Hockey Association (later began NHL)
CHA: Canadian Hockey Association
Sr. MMHL: Senior Montreal Manufacturers Hockey League
Sask-Pro: Saskatoon Professional Hockey League
Sr. XG: Saskatoon Exhibition League

POST HOCKEY CAREER
- **1922** - Secretary-Treasurer Raymore and District, Sask, (Worked in the Raymore lumber business.) Moved to Vancouver, B.C. in 1922 and played for the British Columbia Electric baseball team.
- **1925** – Manager - St. Augustine "Stags" baseball - Vancouver B.C. Amateur "B" champs. (Son, Larry, was the pitcher).
- **1930?** – Coach, Knights of Columbus baseball – Manager. (Sons Leo and Eddie were on the team).
- **1932** – Coach, Firemen's Hockey Team (Local No. 18) – Commercial League Champions. Winners of the Home Oil Distributors trophy. (Son, Larry, was on the team. Son, Roy, was the "mascot.")

(1) Per the Manitoba Hockey Hall of Fame.
(2) This was the very first professional league.
(3) Holden joined the Wanderers for the remainder of the 1907-08 season once the Maple Leafs were out of contention for the Stanley Cup.
He was hired to help the team defeat Ottawa in a game that was to decide the "destination of the Stanley Cup." The Wanderers

and Ottawa were tied for the Eastern League Championship at the time.

(4) The NHA became the NHL

(5) Winnipeg Victorias – According to "From Prairie Wool to Golden Grain" Raymore Saskatchewan & District, 1904-1979.

(a) All-Star - second team

(b) All-Star - second team

(c) All-Star - first team

* Captain

Notes: It has been stated that he played for the Ottawa Silver Seven, however no evidence exists to substantiate that claim.

TABLE OF CONTENTS

FOREWORD   VII

INTRODUCTION   X I

BARNEY HOLDEN (TEAM HISTORY)   XIV

CHAPTER 1 A Winnipeg Childhood   1

CHAPTER 2 Portage Lakes & The .H.L.   7

CHAPTER 3 Winnipeg Maple Leafs   37

CHAPTER 4 Montreal Shamrocks   41

CHAPTER 5 Quebec Bulldogs   59

CHAPTER 6 Saskatoon Wholesalers, and beyond   67

CHAPTER 7 One Last Game   71

EPILOGUE   a) Whatever Happened to...?   78
             b) Hockey Card Collecting   98
             c) Barney Holden:
                  Individual Career Statistics   102

ABOUT THE AUTHOR   104

BIBLIOGRAPHY   105

CHAPTER 1

A WINNIPEG CHILDHOOD

"...the Canadian winter sports scene (reflected) the ingenuity of the vigorous nineteenth century inhabitants of this northern land."

- Allan Cox, "History of Sports in Canada"

Since 1738 there were fur trading posts on the site of what would eventually become known as Winnipeg, Manitoba. No one could imagine that only 150 years later, Manitoba would supply the world with some of the greatest hockey players in the world.

The first permanent settlement of the area of Winnipeg occurred in 1812 when a group of Scottish "crofters" arrived, but it wouldn't be until 1873 when Winnipeg would be incorporated as a city with a population of 1,869 people. The arrival of the Canadian Pacific Railway in 1885 brought a 30-year period of growth and prosperity unequalled in Canadian urban development. A flood of immigrants, high wheat prices, and improved farming techniques contributed to making Winnipeg the wholesale, administrative, and financial center of western Canada. It wasn't long before these hearty folks turned their energies to recreation during the long winter months.

It was during this flourishing economic time that Bernard "Barney" Holden was born on March 21, 1881. His father, Patrick, was a successful contractor from Montreal, Quebec and a member of the Ancient Order of Hibernians, an Irish-Catholic fraternal organization. He had relocated the family to Winnipeg hoping to capitalize on the rapid growth and to expand his contracting business. Not much was known about Barney's mother, Ellen Duggan, other than she was born in Ireland, and in keeping with 18th-19th Century Irish naming traditions, Barney was named after her father, Bernard Duggan. "Barney" is the most common nickname, and thus Bernard Holden became known as "Barney." Patrick Holden, Barney's father, was a larger than life character. A huge, balding, barrel-chested fellow...the type of chap you would imagine stepping out of an old John Ford movie. When he died in Winnipeg, in 1912, his obituary stated:

> "Patrick Holden was one of the most powerful men physically in the west and acted as anchor man on the old Irish tug-of-war team when it successfully overcame all comers in that sport."

One can almost envision the tug-of-war competitions in late 1800's Quebec that would pit ethnic groups against one another... all for the right to claim who was the strongest. Apparently the scrappy Irish did very well.

Patrick had been raised in Shannon, Quebec, on the muddy banks of the Riviere Jacques Cartier. There was a large Irish community at the time, thriving in the separatist heartland of French Quebec. Many of the Irish, like Patrick's father, Daniel, crossed the North Atlantic in the 1820's from Cos. Kilkenny, Wexford, and Carlow to homestead on the wild banks of the Riviere Jacques Cartier, which Irish locals still insist on calling the "Jackarty." Prior to the 1820s, 2/3rds of the Irish landing in Quebec, Nova Scotia, and New Brunswick continued traveling until they reached the U.S. After 1816, new British Passenger Acts temporarily reduced the volume and altered the direction of Irish emigration to British North America. For the next two decades most of the Irish sailed in the holds of Canadian Timber ships to Quebec or the Maritime Provinces. Nevertheless, despite Parliament's intentions, before 1819 relatively few Irish actually settled in Canada, conditions were too primitive, employment was scarce, speculators monopolized much of the available land, and most Irish preferred to follow kinfolk who had previously emigrated to the United States where work was steady. However, in 1819, the government of Upper Canada (now called Ontario) began giving 50 acres land grants to attract settlers. In the same year, reports of financial panic and economic depression in the U.S. began to reach Ireland. To the Irish in the early 1820s, Canada appeared to offer a better life than the states.

By 1827 the British had repealed all restrictions on emigration and over 20,000 Irish responded to lower fares and potential prosperity. 65% of the emigrating Irish sailed to British provinces, primarily Quebec. While the great Irish exodus has always been associated with the great cities in the eastern United States, who fled cruel poverty and brutal English rule, many people do not realize that a huge number of Irish also streamed into the St. Lawrence River ports of Quebec City and Montreal, and then spread out to the tiny farms in the Quebec countryside. In the 1851 Quebec census, every county in Ireland was represented by the new inhabitants. Passage to Quebec was cheaper than to the Boston, New York, or Philadelphia, and the fact that the French Canadians were also Catholics was certainly an enticement. So the Irish poured into British North America by the tens of thousands, and changed the face of Montreal forever. The city's flag still bears the Irish harp (along with the English rose, French fleur-de-lys, and Scottish thistle.) The Montreal St. Patrick's Day parade, a tradition since 1824, is rivaled only by the parades of Boston and New York. Over the many decades that followed the Irish emigration into Quebec, the Irish were mostly absorbed into the French culture, keeping their surnames but surrendering the English language and much of their Gaelic identity. As a note, this has not been the case for the 1,850 current residents of Shannon, the descendents of the original Irish, who have remained "a true Irish enclave in the mostly French region in North America." Even to this day they are called, "Les Irlandais du Quebec," (The Quebec Irish.)

The Holdens of Co. Wexford, who eventually put down roots in Montreal, were an off-shoot of a Welsh family called *Houlyn* who settled in Co. Kilkenny following the Anglo-Norman invasion at the end of the twelfth century. There were many early variants of the name such as *Holying, Houlyn, Houlin* and *Howling,* and these eventually became known as *Howlin.* The Howlins eventually spread into the Walsh Mountains on the border of Cos. Kilkenny and Wexford and began calling themselves the Anglican sounding name of *Holden.* It was from that clan that Barney descended.

Barney's paternal grandfather, Daniel Holden, was born in Co. Wexford, Ireland in 1810. He immigrated to Montreal, Quebec (Shannon) around 1830 with his wife, Mary (Fitzpatrick) where they raised several children, including Patrick, who was born in 1844. Catholicism played a pivotal, if not all-consuming role in their lives of the Holden clan, as it did for most Irish immigrants of the time.

Perhaps the best example of how the faith dominated the family can be explained in a story about Barney's Aunt Margaret, the sister of Patrick Holden. Daniel and Mary (Fitzpatrick) Holden lived next door to the Meagher family (pronounced "Marr") in the St. Gabriel de Valcartier parish in Quebec County, Canada East (as that part of Montreal was known then). Since travel was limited, it was not uncommon for neighbors to marry neighbors, and so Margaret Holden, the daughter of Daniel and Mary Holden, eventually married Edward "Ned the Fiddler" Meagher (who would later spell his name as "Maher") on December 28, 1868. Ned was a gifted musician, but could neither read nor write. He had arrived in Quebec from Co. Tipperary with his parents in the spring of 1832. Together, Ned and Mary (Holden) Maher would raise their nine children as good Catholics, including their oldest son and first child, Daniel "Herbert" Maher, born 1870, and named after his grandfather. Over the years Daniel grew to be a fine-looking lad and eventually was employed as a Street-Car Conductor in Bay City, Michigan, where the family had relocated years before to operate an apple farm. For some reason, perhaps as an act of rebellion, Daniel began to spell his name *Mahar,* while his brothers and sisters kept the old spelling of *Maher.*

Then, in 1894, Daniel shocked his parents by announcing his marriage to an Elizabeth Krack...*a Methodist.* The marriage to a protestant was not received well at all by his Catholic parents, as one would imagine. But even more devastating was the announcement that he was leaving the Catholic faith to join the Methodist Church. Despite his parent's misgivings, Daniel and Elizabeth would go on to raise seven children in the Methodist faith, and remain relatively unfettered by the Catholic Holden clan.

In 1913, as Daniel was helping to repair the roof of the Methodist church, he lost his footing, tumbled off the roof, and fell to the ground. He died instantly. He was only 43 years old and he left behind a widow and seven children. Immediately, his mother seized the opportunity. Viewing this tragedy as a sign from God that Daniel had turned his back on Catholicism, and before her son's body was even cold, Mary Holden-Maher (now known as "Granny" Maher) snatched up Daniel's two youngest children and whisked them off to be re-baptized in the Catholic Church. Mary later explained her impulsive actions by stating, "I did it because that way the Methodists could not have any claim to them." In her eyes, she had saved two of her grandchildren from eternal damnation.

What is interesting is that Barney, probably not knowing what had occurred in Michigan USA, would find himself in the very same situation as his cousin, Daniel Mahar (without falling off the roof) when he himself married a Methodist girl, Mary Wilkinson,. She wasn't just your ordinary Irish-protestant lass, but the daughter of the past-president of a Loyal Orange Lodge (an anti-Catholic, pro-British organization, also known as the "Orangemen.") While this marriage probably didn't thrill Barney's family, it is safe to assume that Big Jim Wilkinson most certainly did not embrace it. Barney was smart, however, and remained out of the Wilkinson family fray. Hopefully he was far away when Mary announced to her parents that she intended to convert to Catholicism in order to marry an *Irish-Catholic hockey player!* In those days, that was tantamount to marrying a circus performer. Only an actor (or perhaps a baseball player) might have ranked lower on the food chain than a hockey player.

But other than Barney's oldest son, Larry, once getting caught in the middle of an ideological feud between his dogmatic grandfathers, no lives were lost, no serious damage was done, and life continued as normal. The feud between the *Orange* (James Wilkinson) and the *Green* (Patrick Holden) eventually subsided. Perhaps love did triumph overall.

Let's back up a wee bit. In the big prairie town of Winnipeg, Manitoba around the 1890's, Barney Holden, like most of the young boys, grew up learning to skate and play baseball. Both sports were in their relative infancy, having only been introduced to Manitoba within the last 10 years or so. In his early teens he spent his summers playing for the Union Baseball Club, and in the winters he played hockey for various amateur teams including the St. Mary's Septette, Canadian Pacific Railroad, and the Winnipeg Telegram.

His Union Baseball Club made history on August 28, 1899 when they played the female American softball champions, the Boston Bloomer Girls, at Fort Garry Park in Winnipeg. The boys lost. In fairness to the Union club, it was well known that a few male "ringers" always played with the girls. During the same year, the Winnipeg Telegram hockey team ended their 1899 season undefeated. Perhaps they should have challenged the Bloomer Girls to a hockey match instead. Only St. Boniface would give the Telegram team a run for their money, but they still lost to the Telegram, 3-2.

One of Barney's teammates that year was Joe Wilkinson, a pug-looking Irish-protestant whose family hailed from Co. Tyrone in the north of Ireland. It was Joe who introduced Barney to his sister, Mary, who would eventually become his wife. Sadly, Joe would be among the many Canadian casualties of the Battle of Vimy Ridge in World War I. He had been assigned to the First Winnipeg Mounted Rifles (Saskatchewan Division) and was killed by German shellfire. He managed to hang on for a few days, but eventually succumbed to his wounds on April 12, 1918. This was quite a blow to Mary who had already lost a younger sister to consumption.

CHAPTER TWO

PORTAGE LAKES & THE I.H.L.

"...the stand of the Ontario Hockey Association against professionalism...must be uncompromisingly antagonistic... Any player who figures on any of these teams must be banished from Ontario Hockey!"

- John Robinson, Ontario Hockey Association, 1904

Prior to WWI, amateur hockey was at the peak of its popularity in Winnipeg, but also still in its formative years. According to the *Hockey Canada* website, the origin of hockey in Canada has never been definitely established. Several claims have been made on behalf of many towns and cities, most notably Montreal, Halifax and Kingston. Early in the development of the game of Ice Hockey, people who loved to skate were referred to as *skatists*. When the game of Ice Hockey began to catch on, those playing the game became referred to as *Hockeyists*.

Early organizers had no plans to develop an international league of teams made up of the highest paid players in North America. They were only interested in the love of a new game that attracted boys and young men and helped to fill the time during the long, cold Canadian winters. There is no doubt that hockey had been played for a long time in Canada, and individual clubs such as the Victorias of Montreal were known at an early date. Montreal also lays claim to having the first organized league of clubs. However, hockey didn't arrive in Winnipeg until 1890's according to the *birthplaceofhockey.com*. So at a time when most Manitoba kids are learning to play the game, turning professional was the last thing a player envisioned, in fact, it wasn't even an option. That all changed in 1903 when the Portage Lakers were formed in Houghton, Michigan, USA.

According to historian Daniel Scott Mason, the first "openly-acknowledged" professional ice hockey team actually played its first game in Houghton, Michigan, USA in 1901, but it wasn't until 1903 when Houghton would organize the very first professional hockey team. The town of Houghton could not have been a better choice for the birthplace of professional hockey. This was a copper-rich town where the local miners loved to blow off steam by imbibing and watching aggressive hockey on a Saturday night. It was a flourishing community of about 5,000 souls at the time, and was located in the northern most part of the state, between Portage Lake and Lake Superior.

Houghton had already undergone a professional baseball craze in which they resorted to paying players up to $225 in order to secure the Upper Peninsula championship. Local entrepreneurs envisioned doing the same with ice hockey. Merv Youngs, a cub reporter for the Houghton Daily Mining Gazette, had discovered that their local dentist, John L. "Doc" Gibson had been a standout hockey player for his native Berlin, Ontario, and Youngs convinced Gibson to organize a professional team. Since the inhabitants of Houghton, Michigan, U.S.A. didn't really know how to play the game, Gibson had to recruit from Canada who had embraced the game whole-heartedly a decade before.

At the time, the Canadian amateur hockey associations had adamantly discouraged professional hockey, and some players, no doubt, wrestled with the morality of being a hired gun. Others had no problem being paid to play a game they loved, and were already playing for free anyway. So while the Canadians were really puckered over the emergence of professional hockey, even calling it "disgusting," the Americans were less judgmental, they just wanted to see good hockey in a regular league season and be able to watch games every weekend. And since Houghton winters can bring up to 300 inches of snow, winter sports had always been vital to the community for commerce and entertainment.

On top of that, Houghton was a very rich community as all of the copper mines were still functioning and the demand for copper was at a record high. They had the money, they had the demand, and Gibson had the connections because of his playing days in Canada. It seemed like a logical business decision. So Gibson accepted the challenge, and with the financial backing from local businessmen, he began openly advertising in Canada, and elsewhere, for hockey players to come to Houghton, Michigan, U.S.A. and play for pay. Thus, Gibson began to organize the first "fully-fledged professional hockey team" that would challenge any team, amateur or professional.

Nicknamed the "Portage Lakers," they were named for the navigable body of water in the Keeweenaw Peninsula which juts into Lake Superior. In the fall of 1903, Gibson visited Canada in an effort to observe and recruit professional players. Future great "Riley" Hern and "Hod" Stuart were enlisted, as was his brother, Bruce, along with "Cooney" Shields, Bert Morrison, and Ernie Westcott.

This move into "professional hockey" was a very historic and controversial event in sports history. The Canadians were appalled, and reacted by banning the players from ever playing in Canada again. Canadian amateur hockey enthusiasts were certain the Americans were trying to ruin their national sport. Regardless, from 1904-1907, the best players in Manitoba would be lured across the border into the United States to play for money.

In 1904, as quoted in the Copper Country Evening News, John Ross Robertson of the OHA was reported to have said "for self preservation, the stand of the Ontario Hockey Association against the professionalism of Pittsburgh, Houghton, Calumet and the Soo must be uncompromisingly antagonistic...Any player who figures on any of these teams must be banished from Ontario Hockey." So while the professional ranks continued to hold no lure for some, enough of the more talented players were heading to the U.S. This was quite a gamble for these young Canucks. If the professional stint in the U.S. didn't work out, they couldn't return to Canada to play. Their options would have been to play amateur hockey in the U.S., which would have been logistically difficult, if not financially impossible, or return to Canada and not be able to play any form of organized amateur hockey. But the chance to be paid to play the sport they loved, and were already playing gratis, was just too much. Besides, the Canadian players were fed-up with the often-disjointed Ontario and Manitoba leagues and felt they had nothing to lose. If those leagues couldn't get their acts together, the Canadians were going to head across the border.

By 1903 there were a number of restless hockey players looking for a home, including Barney Holden. Many had been orphans of the various dysfunctional teams and leagues that would form, shrink, move, change names, reform, fold, and move again. *"Players drifted about the landscape like snowflakes in a lazy prairie breeze,"* according to author Eric Whitehead. Although this was technically a professional team, they could only play exhibition matches as no league had been formed. As one might imagine, each and every game was a slaughter. No team could stand up to what was called *the greatest collection of hockey talent ever assembled.* It was a bit of a joke actually. The fans, loyal though they were, demanded more competitive games. They found the games boring, and wanted to see their boys go head-to-head with the best Canada had to offer. Even "Hod" Stuart, speaking on behalf of his team, wanted to "beat the big Canadian teams on their own ice…"

So in 1904, lead by the success of the original 1903 Portage Lake Hockey Club, entrepreneurs organized the International Hockey League, the first professional hockey league in the world. Scattered around the Manitoba League, the Canadian Amateur Hockey Association (CAHA), and the Federal League were talented characters such as "Ed "Newsy" Lalonde, a crazy Frenchman who loved to fight; Fred "Cyclone" Taylor, the Wayne Gretzky of his day; the Patrick Brothers, Lester and Frank; and "Bad" Joe Hall, his name said it all. Other outstanding

Canadian players looking for a home were Paddy Moran, Tommy Dunderdale, Ernie "Moose" Johnson, and Joe Malone.

The IHL, also referred to as the International Professional Hockey League or International Pro League, consisted of the following teams: Sault St. Marie (Michigan) AKA "Michigan Soo," whose home ice was their local curling rink called the *Ridge Street Ice-A-Torium*; (they were called the "Indians"); Houghton (Michigan) whose home ice in the new Amphidrome on Portage Lake; Calumet (Michigan) with home ice in the new Palastra; Pittsburgh (Pennsylvania) with home ice in the Duquesne Gardens; and Sault St. Marie (Ontario) AKA "Canadian Soo," with home ice at their local curling rink. Even the team colors had to be decided. Pittsburgh would wear the red and blue, Canadian Soo would sport red and black, Michigan Soo would wear purple and white, Houghton would wear green and white, and Calumet would wear a God-awful combination of pearl gray and cardinal (gray jerseys with red stockings). The referees would wear yellow sweaters. Each team then scrambled to recruit the best players they could find.

All of the former Portage Lakers from the 1902-03 team listened to the offers from the newly formed teams, as well as from their former team. The players were paid anywhere from $25 to $75 dollars per week, plus expenses. Depending on whether the player was paid at the higher end of the scale, it could be quite lucrative, considering the average Canadian salary in 1905 was $375, or $31 per week. "Newsey" Lalonde was paid $50 a week. He always said that was much more that the average working stiff at that time. The new the league would operate from approximately December 14 to March 15, depending on the weather. The biggest loss to Houghton was their inability to retain "Hod" Stuart, perhaps the best player in the league at that time. However, they were able to get his brother, Bruce, to return to Houghton as well as all of the original players from the prior year. Local supporters soon adopted nicknames for their teams. Players from the two Soos were called "Lock City Men" (although fans of the American Soo preferred, "Wolverines"), and those from Copper Country (Houghton) were labeled "Miners." Pittsburgh players were called, "Coal Heavers."

The Canadians who were recruited to join the Houghton team noticed immediately that more emphasis was placed on skating and stick-handling than in the Canadian leagues which relied more on brute force. But the Canadians added their influence by placing a quick man to move the puck back up the ice, instead of putting the large man in front of the goaltender. Therefore the goaltender was left to do his job, and the main function of a position called *coverpoint* was to body-check with extreme prejudice. That was exactly the reason they recruited Barney Holden from the Winnipeg Shamrocks, of the Manitoba Northwest Hockey Association. He had the reputation of being a *hitter,* and he was the best choice to replace the great "Hod" Stuart.

Barney had played two years with the Shamrocks where he was one of the Manitoba Northwest Hockey Association standouts. He had the repute of being very physical. At times his play was downright dirty, and he was often used in an enforcer role. His claim to fame was as a very ferocious checker; often crashing into players so hard he could lift them off their skates and send them sprawling across the ice. In short, he was a mean SOB. His father, Patrick, had been a strict disciplinarian who raised his son to be tough. It must have worked as Barney never lost a fight growing up in Winnipeg, and often took out his aggression on the ice. Much to the dismay of his hapless opponents.

As mentioned previously, Holden was a coverpoint, which was basically a defenseman who roamed the ice at will and hustled back to his own end of the ice in time to make defensive plays. So any fellow playing that position had to be very fast. The coverpoint position no longer exists in present day hockey, but in the old days a team consisted of seven players: goal, point and coverpoint (these two being the defensemen, who lined up one in front of the other), rover, center, right wing, and left wing. The goalkeeper was required to stay on his feet at all times. Falling down to block a puck was a violation.

The Portage Lake players were allowed to train at the local Houghton YMCA until the ice became hard and thick enough to be suitable for skating. Sometimes that took days. Often times it was a couple of weeks.

The uniforms and equipment of the day were very rudimentary. By the 1890's, ankle support straps gave the player more stability, replacing the simple skates that attached to the bottom of shoes. In 1904, hockey "gauntlets," or padded gloves, were introduced into the game. They were clumsy and awkward and many players didn't approve at first. But Barney took to them right away. No more busted knuckles. It has been said that short pants and long stocking arrived around 1910, but Barney was wearing the unpadded version long before then. Around 1910 the pads were added, as were knee pads. Shin pads finally arrived in 1912, and goal tenders were finally able to throw away their old cricket pants in exchange for actual goal tender leg pads. The 1920's and 30's would bring even more innovation all in an effort to protect the player. Interestingly enough, shoulder pads didn't arrive until the 1940's. Designed for defensemen, many were reluctant at first, but soon all defensemen strapped on the pads. But defensemen like Barney and "Hod" Stuart never used shoulder pads, or loin pads, shin guards, elbow pads, face-masks, or helmets. Nothing lay between the player and the ice, or the player and the collision of an oncoming foe, but a simple wool turtleneck sweater and a pair of really bad looking shorts.

Newsey Lalonde enjoyed describing his first uniform when he signed on with Sault Ste. Marie of the IHL: "They gave me a pair of rugby pants, a shirt that was too long, some stockings that looked a dozen years old, and skates that would fit an elephant." His uniform experience was similar to many of the IHL players.

Once Holden arrived in Houghton, Michigan, he immediately inspected the famous Amphidrome ice rink that seated 3,000 (of the 5,000 inhabitants of Houghton). It was almost always jammed to capacity for any sports event. Holden was met by League Secretary, John McNamara, a tall Irishman with a large, drooping mustache. McNamara explained that league standings would be based on percentage points, much like baseball, and the team would compete for a "pennant" not for the "championship." This seemed rather complicated to Barney who was used to the much simpler "wins vs. losses" type of competition. But that was the least if his worries. Holden knew he had been recruited to replace the best player in the league, if not the world, and the pressure was on. McNamara was quick to remind him of that fact as well.

On the night of the first game of the season, the fans came in droves to see if this new kid from Manitoba was worthy of filling the void left by the great Stuart. With cow bells clanging and whistles blowing, 4,000 spectators, including many Houghton fans, shouted and screamed their delight during the season opener of the International Hockey League. In his very first game for Portage Lake, Barney didn't disappoint.

PORTAGE LAKES ARE VICTORIOUS

Pittsburg(h) Team Meets Defeat in First Game of Season By Score of 6 to 3

BARNEY HOLDEN MAKES GOOD

Nearly Four Thousand People Witness The Opening Game of the Season in the Smokey City

(Special Telegraphic Service)

"Pittsburg(h), Pa., Dec. 9 – Portage Lake opened the International Hockey League season tonight at Duquesne Garden by winning from the Pittburg(h) team by a score of 6 to 3."

Holden Makes Good

"Portage Lake presented the same line up as last year with the exception of Barney Holden instead of Hod Stuart at cover point. Holden is filling the shoes of one of the very best men who was with Portage last season and he seems capable to equal the record of the famous Hod. Holden watches the man closer than he does the puck and he is usually successful in blocking the runner headed toward his goal."

The article then gave a run-down of the performance of the other players, Bruce Stuart "just as fast as ever," and Fred Lake, "the plucky little fellow."

"Holden shot the first goal for Portage on a pass from Shields, who made a long run. Shields shot the second goal from the side of the rink, digging the disc from a scrimmage. Lake scored the third goal for the visitors from scrimmage and Bruce Stuart registered the fourth before the end of the first period on a pass from Holden.

Interest naturally centered on Barney Holden, the new cover point. He was the only untried man on the team. Almost every bulletin gave Barney honorable mention. He scored the first goal and he did some vicious checking, being often penalized."

The Portage Lake fans gathered at the Amphidrome, McKenzie & Foley's, and the Board of Trade to wait for the results of the first game of the season. "An immense crowd was about town waiting for the returns and the enthusiasm when the Portage Lakes were known to be victorious was great."

Line Up of Teams

Portage Lake		Pittsburgh
Hern	G	McKay
Gibson	P	Spittal
Holden	CP	Duval
Morrison	F	Roberts
Stuart	C	Campbell
Shields	RW	Black
Lake	LW	Sixsmith

Goals – Portage: Holden, Stuart, Shields (2), Gibson, Lake; Pittsburgh: Duvall, Campbell, Sixsmith. Attendance – 3,500

Hockey in those days was very different from today. It was played with seven men aside, rather than six. For 30 minutes the players battled on the ice, stopped for a ten minute half-time, and then played another 30 minutes. A defenseman's job was to basically go out on the ice and assault people...try to put them out of the game. Cripple them if necessary. Most players said goodbye to their front teeth years ago, including Barney. Since no substitutions were allowed, if you were injured and had to leave the game, you were not allowed back in. So players never left the ice...unless they were carried off. There was no such thing as a "poke check," they simply chopped your legs out from under you with their stick (slashing was not illegal unless you struck your opponent above the knees). No helmets, little padding, bigger sticks. Imagine the mayhem. Another difference between hockey of yesteryear was the "slapshot." It didn't exist back then. In the early days of hockey there was only the "wrist shot." It was fast and very accurate. Modern day slapshots are powerful, but inaccurate. It is more of a *spray and pray* shot.

Hockey historians will tell you that the game of hockey wasn't invented...it evolved. So determining the exact origin is difficult. It has been said that ice hockey came from English field hockey and Indian lacrosse and was spread throughout Canada by British soldiers in the mid 1800s. That may or may not be true.

For those readers interested in hockey's Irish origins…read on. If not, skip the next few pages. The author won't be offended at all.

One popular view as to the origin of hockey lies in the stick… the Irish *hurley* stick. Many people believe that ice hockey evolved out the Irish field game called hurley which is played year round in Ireland on a field with a ball and stick. The game of hurley was played regularly in the fields of Nova Scotia back in the early 1800's. But when winter came hurley was to difficult to play because of the snow, so the game eventually moved onto the ice. This new game called "Hurley on Ice" started at King's College in Windsor, Nova Scotia just outside of Halifax. In fact, it was men from Cos. Cork and Waterford who began playing ice-hurley, or ice hockey, in Nova Scotia. This theory has been supported by Dave Hanigan of the Irish Sunday Tribune who claims that ice hockey owes it roots to hurling. It was Irishmen who played hurley on a frozen stretch of water known as *The Long Pond* and there is recorded evidence of such a sport taking place in that location before 1844. There is also evidence of hurling games being played by Waterford and Mooncoin (Co. Kilkenny) men in Newfoundland long before the Windsor games took place. It then became very popular on the East Coast for the first 50 years of the 1800's.

As far as the Society of International Hockey Research (SIHR) is concerned, the Windsor claim is merely anecdotal and does not stand up to academic scrutiny, according to John O'Connor of the Munster Express. Rather, the SIHR believes that the first modern game of ice hockey took place in the Victoria skating rink in Montreal, Quebec on March 3, 1875.

Still, no one can explain how the game evolved up to that point. O'Connor suspects that Seamus J. King was right on target in his book, *The Clash of the Ash in Foreign Fields*, when he declared, "so, it seems the first men to have struck a ball in the New World were sons of Waterford helped by Mooncoin men from across the river." (How interesting it is to note that Barney Holden's ancestors still reside in the Mooncoin area of Co. Kilkenny, Ireland).

Other evidence of the early influence of hurley include the word "puck." When a hurley player knocks the ball with his hurley stick, the ball has been "pucked." The word "rink" comes from the Scottish, and it means "race course." When the game started, the goals were actually at the sides of the rink, to avoid long shots scoring by barreling the puck down the ice.

Hurling is very similar to hockey in that it is played with a small ball and a curved wooden stick. It is Europe's oldest field game. When the Celts came to Ireland as the last ice age was receding, they brought with them a unique culture, their own language, music, script, and unique pastimes. One of these pastimes was a game now called hurling. It is featured in Irish folklore to illustrate the deeds of heroic mythical figures like *Cuchulain*, and it is chronicled as a distinct Irish pastime for at least 2,000 years. The stick, or "hurley" (called *caman* in Irish gaelic) is curved outwards at the end to provide the striking surface. The ball, or "sliothar," is similar in size to a hockey ball, but has raised ridges. It is the third most popular sport in Ireland (soccer is second) and is now played by approximately 100,000 Irish people. It remains one of the fastest and most skillful field games in the world.

The earliest written record of the game is contained in the Brehon Laws of the fifth century. The first recorded reference to hurling dates to the Battle of Moytura (*Magh Tuiredh*) near Cong in Co. Mayo (West of Ireland) in 1272 B.C. between the native Fir Bolg (known as "Men of the Bags" from a slave class of earth carriers," or possibly, "Men of the God of Lightning") and the invading Tuatha De Danann ("People of the Danu" or "The People of the Goddess Dana"). As both sides were preparing for battle, someone suggested they conduct a hurling contest instead. Twenty-seven of the best players lined up on both sides and fought a bloody match. In the end, the Fir Bolg were victorious, and they celebrated by slaying the Tuatha De Danann. So much for being a good winner. The game was banned by the Statutes of Kilkenny because of its popularity with the Normans.

One of the earliest references to hurling, and by far the most famous, is from a 12th century document that tells the story of Cuchulainn, a Herculean type of hero, and clearly mentions the word *camán* which is the Irish word for *hurley*. Cuchulainn (aka Setanta) was an Irish hero/god whose story parallels Hercules. Born of a human father (Sualtam) and an unknown women who may have been be a goddess, he had a spiritual father-son relationship with the god, Lugh. He studied under the warrior goddess, Scathach, and returned to Ulster as a great warrior. He led the Red Branch, a band of warriors whose exploits are related in one of the cycles in Irish mythology. Cuchulainn is honored as a pagan god and became semi-divine through his adventures. The Book of the Dun Cow recorded many of his stories. Cuchulainn was one of the greatest Irish mythological heroes and legend tells us of his famous feat when, as a young boy, known then as Setanta, defeated a viscous hound by hitting his ball through the mouth of the hound with his hurley. This story is told in Táin Bo Cuailgne (The Cattle Raid of Cooley). The legend, which was revived from extinction by Sechan Torpeist, a 7th century bard, tells the story of how Setanta, the nephew of King Conchobair Mac Neasa of Ulster, receives the name of Cuchulainn:

> Setanta journeys to his uncle's court to join the boy's corps. He shortened his walk by hurling his silver sliotar (ball) and then throwing his bronze hurley stick after it. He would run and catch both the sliotar and the hurley stick before they hit the ground. Soon he arrived at court, and his hurling abilities amazed the boys of the corps. Legend has it that he was able to score with ease and when he guarded the goal he never let a shot in.

One day King Conchobair was invited to a banquet at the house of Culainn (there are several different spellings of his name) and asked his nephew to join him. Setanta agreed to go after he finished playing a hurling game. While at the feast Culainn asked the king if all the guests had arrived. King Conchobair, forgetting about Setanta, said yes and Culainn unleashed his hound to guard the house. When Setanta arrived at the feast the great hound leapt up to attack him, but Setanta quickly hurled the sliotar at the hound and it went down the beast's throat. The boy immediately grabbed the stunned hound by his feet and smashed its head into the floor of the stone courtyard killing him.

When the guests heard the baying of the hound they ran outside and were surprised to see Setanta alive and the beast dead. King Conchobair was overjoyed but Culainn was sad at the loss of his favorite hound. Setanta offered to find a hound worthy of the one he had slain and vowed to guard Culainn's home until such an animal could be found. Thus Setanta became known as Cuchulainn, which translates to "the hound of Culainn".

Hurling was also a common way to train warriors for battle. Even the Vikings tried their hand at the sport before Brian Boru and his Irish warriors sent them packing.

The website "Birthplace of Hockey" also supports the Irish connection:

"[Ice Hockey] originated around 1800, in Windsor, where the boys of Canada first college, King's College School, established in 1788, adapted the exciting field game of Hurley to the ice of their favorite skating ponds and originated a new winter game, Ice Hurley. Over a period of decades, Ice Hurley gradually developed into Ice Hockey."

The heel of a hurley stick is virtually identical in angle to a present-day ice hockey stick. Researchers are confident the hurley stick had been adapted to ice hockey, lengthening both the blade and the handle. Between 1800 and 1860, hurley on ice spread rapidly across the province as immigrants from Great Britain and Ireland landed in Eastern Canada. They referred to the game as either *hurley on ice*, *wicket* or *ricket* (referring to the goal posts) and eventually newspaper reports began calling the game "hockey."

In the early forms of Ice Hockey, a player was not allowed to pass the puck forward. This made the game like English Rugby Football. However, in order to speed up the play, this rule was gradually withdrawn. Now, Hockey resembles International Football (Soccer) in this respect.

Ice hockey may have developed from the Scottish game of *shinty*, but it is well known that shinty evolved from hurling. Irish missionaries introduced it to Scotland, along with the Gaelic language, approximately 2,000 years ago. Anyone who knows the history of Scotland knows that it was originally an Irish kingdom. The terms *Scotia* and *Scot* were first applied to Ireland and Irishmen, but later came to be applied to Ireland's northeastern neighbor, Alba (Scotland) and its inhabitants. More than missionaries relocated to Scotland. So it is no stretch to assume that the migrating Irish brought the game of hurley to Scotland. The Scots then put their unique stamp on the game and called it *shinty*. But it was still an Irish game!

It's easy to speculate when the first organized hockey game probably took place. That appears to have occurred in the town of Windsor, Nova Scotia. Thomas Haliburton was born in Windsor in 1796 and attended King's College School. He would become a judge and a writer in his later years. It was one of his writings that provided Windsor with its self-proclaimed title as the "birthplace of hockey." Haliburton wrote an article in 1844 about his childhood memories of "boys (playing) hurley on the Long Pond on the ice." There are others who claim the first games occurred in Halifax, or at McGill University in Montreal, Quebec. It is certainly possible they occurred simultaneously.

Many variations of the game were played before the definitive version of the game evolved and was eventually embraced by all Canadians. Research then showed that a game similar to hockey was played in the early 1800s in Nova Scotia by the Micmac Indians who were heavily influenced by the Irish game of hurley.

From the games played in the early 1800's in Windsor, hockey spread to Quebec by 1875, then into Kingston, Ontario in 1886, and south to Toronto in 1888. By 1890, the game had arrived in Winnipeg, and then extended to Victoria, British Columbia becoming a coast-to-coast Canadian game.

Anyway, back to the early 20th century. Historians are quick to point out that the International Hockey League was one of the roughest leagues ever conceived. Perhaps the violence was fueled by greed, as the best players could demand the larger salaries. Over the next three years the league was in existence, it tried to deal with the violence by attempting to ban "Hod" Stuart and "Bad" Joe Hall for their rough play and "homicidal tendencies." In fairness to the league, many of the reports of violence were exaggerated by the "flash writers" (Canadian sports writers) in an effort to prove that professional hockey was barbaric and not at all the gentlemen's sport as it was in the provinces. The reports of violence were not unfounded. It was a very vicious league. The players were smaller and the ice slower, so body-checking didn't have the same bone-crushing effect as in today's hockey. Daniel Mason stated the repertoire of the I.H.L. player were mostly cross-checking, high-sticking, and slashing. More like sword-play. Modern day hockey is a cross between a ballet and a Central Park mugging. But it was rough, make no mistake about it. The Houghton miners loved it, but some townsfolk were certain they would eventually witness a man murdered on the ice. Unfortunately, that would occur in the Canadian Federal Amateur Hockey League in 1907 when Owen "Bud" McCourt of the Cornwall team would sustain fatal injuries in a game against the Ottawa Victorias in what had been described as "…a rumble, a gang fight on ice and a homicide," according to *HockeyWeekly.com*. Several Ottawa players were brought up on murder charges, but since they couldn't really tell how many players had struck McCourt, or when during the game he was struck, the charges were dropped.

Normally, hockey violence at that time was spontaneous and fleeting. Only rarely did it evolve in an ugly spectacle between two or more players, as it did between McCourt and the Ottawa players.

On one occasion during the 1905-06 season, Pittsburgh player, "Hod" Stuart and Michigan Soo player, Paul "Pud" Hamilton, locked themselves in the dressing room at half time to finish the fight they started in the first half. Even brothers Bruce and "Hod" Stuart were known to go at each other on the ice. For some, the rough play was too much to stomach.

Ken Mallen was a very fast and extremely skilled Calumet player, but he was small compared to the others in the league. He was targeted for extermination at nearly every game because of his size and skill level, and was left unconscious on more than one occasion. He eventually hung up his skates stating he was fed up with the unnecessary violence in the IHL and the fact that the league didn't seem to care. Of course they didn't care. The more violent, the more the seats were filled. Even though the league adopted the rules of the Quebec Hockey Union, the regulations were lax, and in some cases when the referees did respond, they were forced to make up rules in the middle of the game in order to control bad behavior. But that didn't curtail the brutality.

The boards around the rink were generally low in the early 1900s; occasionally a puck would fly into the crowd and smack an unsuspecting fan. Sometimes the puck was sent into the crowd as a way to delay the game, hopefully without the intent to injure a spectator. "Lifting" was another form of sending the puck airborne, and was Barney's particular claim to fame. There was no "icing" rule back then that stated the puck must remain on the ice at all times. Often Barney, while laying back on the defense, would "lift" (also referred to as "laze") the puck high into the air towards the opponents goal. The lighting was often dim, and the numerous colorful banners that hung from the rafters made locating the flying puck quite a challenge. Often the forwards "would skate themselves dizzy" trying to position themselves as the puck descended, and on more than on occasion a goalie would still be looking for a puck that had already found the back of the net. It was Barney's job to monitor his team's fatigue level. If they were running out of gas, he knew it was time to start *lifting* the puck to save energy. If he could get the puck in the air, and down the ice, perhaps one of the forwards could tap it in the net. It wasn't long before the other teams caught on to Barney's sky-high shot. "Newsey" Lalonde said he would wait for guys like Holden to set up for such a shot, and then he'd charge the defender, crashing into him like a football player and stopping his puck-in-the-air shot. A "lifter" had to be quick, or risk getting mowed down.

The inaugural year of the IHPL was deemed a success. The players were young, wild, and reckless, and it was evidenced in the way they played. Part way through the season, Joe Hall once "commandeered" a hansom cab when the Portage team realized they had missed the trolley to their hotel. Partly due to impatience, and also to celebrate Canadian heavyweight boxer Tommy Burns' defeat of Marvin Hart, Hall knocked aside the cabbie and had a grand time speeding through the cobblestones streets of Pittsburgh sending terrified citizens diving out of the way. Barney, and a few other players still in the cab with Hall, simply held on for their lives, laughing with delight and screaming in terror at the same time. The second cab containing the rest of team trotted quite a distance behind them.

The other memorable event that occurred during the first year was when baseball great, Honus Wagner, showed up for one of the last Houghton games against Pittsburgh. The crowd cheered the Pittsburgh Pirate shortstop who was reportedly a huge hockey fan. Wagner had heard about the exciting games being played in the new International Hockey League and traveled from his home in Plattsville to see the game.

Anyway, the triumph of the first year was proof that for owners with enough passion, and cash, and with players tough enough to do anything to win, they could build exciting teams that would bring in droves of fans.

HOUGHTON 1904-05

Every player in the IHL received a salary and some were also given lucrative jobs in the community. "Hod" Stuart, from Ottawa, Ontario, was paid $1,800 by Calumet to play for the team and manage their rink for the 1904-05 season. At the end of the 1904-05 season the Portage Lakers sent word to the Stanley Cup Committee Board of Governors challenging the Ottawa Silver Seven to a championship. The Stanley Cup had been introduced in Canada in 1893 and was to be awarded to the best amateur team in North America. Determined to keep hockey an amateur sport, the Portage Lakers were denied the opportunity to play for the Cup. No way would a professional team be allowed to compete for the cup!

As most of the players only stayed for the two-month season, all of the players then went home, and recruiting had to start all over again for the next season. In essence, the team had to be totally rebuilt each year. Other teams in the new International Hockey Leagues were vying for the better players as well, so the players joined whatever team offered them the most money. They were paid to play for the 3+ month season; then they went home to their families and regular jobs in the spring. The roster for the 1904-05 season included the following: Bruce Stuart, Fred Lake, Bert Morrison, Harry Bright, Barney Holden, Charles Lifton, William "Cooney" Shields, Lorne Campbell, Dr. J. L. "Doc" Gibson, Joe McMaster, C. Ernest "Ernie" Westcott, Andy Haller, and "Riley" Hern. Despite a valiant effort, Portage came in second to the Calumet-Larium Miners. This was quite a coup for Calumet to beat the team that gave birth to the IHL. It was

time for the Portage Lakers to regroup if they intended on taking
the championship the next season.

1905 International Pro Hockey League

	GP	W	L	T	GF	GA	PTS
*Calumet-Larium Miners	24	18	5	1	131	75	37
Houghton-Portage Lakes	24	15	7	2	98	81	32
Michigan Soo Indians	24	10	13	1	81	79	21
Pittsburgh Pro HC	24	8	15	1	82	114	17
Canadian Soo	24	6	17	1	97	140	13

HOUGHTON 1905-06

In December, just prior to start of his second season with
Houghton, Barney and Mary Wilkinson were married. The
Houghton, Michigan and Winnipeg, Manitoba papers printed
several articles about the November 20, 1905 nuptials.

BARNEY HOLDEN'S WEDDING DAY

"One of Winnipeg's best known athletes will join
the benedicts today in the person of Barney Holden
who is to wed Miss Mary Wilkinson. After the
ceremony the young couple will take the train for
Houghton, Michigan where Barney plays hockey
with the professional league team. Locally, Holden is
better known as a baseball player. He has been long
identified with the Unions, and the members of the
latter club took advantage of the happy occasion to
make an address and presentation to one of their most
deserving players. The gift consisted of a handsome
mirrored, quarter-oak music cabinet."

BARNEY HOLDEN HERE

Portage Lake's Famous Cover Point
Arrives in Houghton

"Late Tuesday night, Mr. And Mrs. Barney Holden arrived here from St. Paul Minn., where they have been spending their honeymoon. Mr. and Mrs. Holden were expected to arrive a day sooner, but the heavy storms so tied up the traffic in Northern Minnesota that all trains were delayed several hours and connections could not be made. Local hockeyites will be delighted to know of Barney's arrival as he has been the general favorite for the past two years. In fact, Barney is the favorite coverpoint of the league, for he certainly "is all there" on the ice, and can handle a stick accordingly. He is liked for the fast game he plays and for his gentlemanly manners at all times."

The 1905-06 season turned out to be a close championship race between three towns. It was so close that several proprietors of Houghton hotels and saloons installed private telephones that could receive direct reports from the Amphidrome. Dunns Brothers of Fifth Street, stated that the scores of all games would be announced wherever the Portage Lakers played. Fred "Cyclone" Taylor, who would later become the greatest player of this era, was paid $400 to join the squad six games into the 1905-06 season. Despite a late start, Taylor performed well scoring 11 goals in the half-dozen matches. Already on the team prior to Taylor joining were Joe Hall, Fred Lake, Bruce Stuart, Barney Holden, Harry Bright, "Grindy" Forrester, and Walter Forrest. It was a slightly smaller team than the previous year. "Doc" Gibson chose to referee rather than play this season, and logged 21 games.

In a game against the Canadian Soo, in which Portage won 4-2, (giving them a record of eight wins and three losses, for a percentage of .727) the Lakes had to contend with the Canadian Soo star, Edouard "Newsey" Lalonde, a scrappy little Frenchman who loved to torment the opposition. When asked about Newsy, Fred Taylor once stated, "He'd come at you with fists, elbows, and skates, trying to incite. He was rough, all right." Newsy had scored both goals for the Soo in this particular game, after first smacking "Grindy" Forrester and Barney Holden across the face with his stick. Forrester was struck the first time, and that set the stage. When Holden was struck a few minutes later, he went after Newsy, causing a major free-for-all that had all of the local inebriated miners jumping out of their seats and roaring with delight. Even after the game Newsy went looking for action. He found a local pub, bought drinks for the crowd, sang off-color French-Canadian folk songs, and then beat up a traveling salesman. This was a very tough league. Another nasty character was "Bad" Joe Hall. It was said that when Hall had you in his sights, he'd come at you "using his fists like hatchets." To his teammates, Joe wasn't really that "bad." To the opposition, he was very intimidating. Over his long career, "Bad" Joe Hall would log more penalty minutes that any player in history. That alone would scare the heck out of anyone.

There was one game in particular that Fred Taylor recounted in his autobiography, *Cyclone Taylor: A Hockey Legend* by Eric Whitehead. Taylor explained that one of the negative issues in the IHL were the shady hometown referees who did anything they could to give their own boys a break. Just such a situation occurred one night in a game at Calumet. The Calumet team was struggling with only three wins in the last seven contests. They were very eager for win number four. One of the referees, who later admitted he had been drinking heavily at the local bar thanks to a friendly barkeep, claimed that Calumet had slipped in a goal against Portage Lake. The Houghton team was furious. No way did that puck make it in the goal. But their protests fell on deaf ears. Later in the game, still fuming from the bad call,

Joe Hall swung an elbow and sent a Calumet player sliding into the boards. Hall was ejected, but refused to leave, and motioned for his Portage team mates to come to his aid. While Taylor, Holden, Lake, and the rest of the team proceeded to skate over toward Hall, Joe decided to tell the local crowd what he thought of them and their lousy hometown referees. Basically, he told them where they could stick their rink. Not a good move. The Calumet players were outraged, and they scrambled out and attacked the Portage team, aided by several dozen Calumet fans that slipped and slid their way onto the ice like drunken sailors on shore leave. Rink officials eventually halted the skirmish and play resumed. But not more than a minute later another mysterious goal was scored by the Calumet team. Fuming mad, Portage Captain Bruce Stuart called his team to the center of the ice. "Boys," he said, "that's enough. We're going home." The entire team agreed and began to skate for the exit. Unfortunately, their early departure was thwarted by a huge mod of enraged Calumet fans who met them at the exit waving clubs, sticks, and chairs. They dared the Houghton team to leave the ice. The Portage team froze in their tracks…except Hall. He decided to take on the crowd and skated into their midst. But when he just missed getting brained by a descending 2x4, he quickly retreated and rejoined his team. "Boys," said Captain Stuart after quickly assessing the situation, "maybe we were a little hasty. Let's go back and play a while longer." They returned and finished the game under duress. No goals were logged the rest of the game. Not even mysterious ones. The local Calumet paper saluted their home team by stating they had a "hard-earned triumph…"

The IHL championship came down to the wire in 1906. As teams were eliminated, the "eliminated" teams offered to give their best players to the teams still in contention, all in an effort to defeat Houghton. The ruse failed, and Houghton finished the league one game ahead of Michigan Soo and thus winning the I.H.L. championship. The Houghton Mining Gazette recorded the February 1906 game that sealed the championship for Houghton:

LAST HOCKEY GAME TONIGHT

Portage Lakes and Calumets in Final
Battle on the Ice

The Portage Lakes and Calumets met last night in the Palestra in the first of a two-game series to terminate the season of the International Hockey league.

The teams lined up as follows:

Portage Lake		Calumet
Regan	goal	Nicholson
Taylor	point	Corbean
Holden	coverpoint	"Tuf" Bellefuille
Cochran	rover	Mallen
Stuart	center	Morrison
Lake	left wing	Bellefuille
Forrester	right wing	McDonald

> "The Lakes lost, Calumet winning out by the score of 11 to 3. The game tonight should draw a big crowd as it will give the Portage Lake public the last opportunity to see its team in action. This is admittedly the greatest hockey aggregation ever gathered in the United States…"

The Calumet fans, thirsty for a repeat championship, had developed a rather nasty reputation, as evidenced previously. They harassed and taunted opposing players every chance they had. Most teams were a little scared to play in the Calumet arena. But unruly fans didn't help the Calumet cause, as they ended up next to last by the end of the season, only winning seven games.

To celebrate the first championship for Houghton, the Quincy Band met the new champions at the train depot, and a battery of U.S. Army artillery was perched on the top of a boxcar with its cannon "covering the train's approach to the village" and firing booming *welcome home* volleys. They were proclaimed not only the International League champions, but (unofficially) the champions of the world. The players fell in behind the band, followed by throngs of well-wishers patting them on the backs, and the parade wound its way through the green and white decorations of Sheldon Street to a banquet held at Douglass House.

Appeals had gone out previously to all "factories, foundries, and other such establishments in the area" to blow their whistles when the steam train arrived. And they did. Led by the shrill steam siren on Caroll's Foundry, the other mills and factories joined it to create a deafening sound that could be heard for miles. The Houghton Gazette reported that "more than half the town was at the depot yesterday to watch the heroes of Pittsburgh alight from their train..." To this day, hockey historians have a tough time recalling a more colorful and enthusiastic scene from the old days.

The 1906 International League's All Star Team included four Portage players: Barney Holden, Fred Taylor, Stuart, Fred Lake.

"Barney Holden, coverpoint of the Portage Lakes, will leave tomorrow morning for his home in Winnipeg. Holden's wife and baby boy are waiting for him, and he will be on his way just as soon as the last time keeper's whistle of the season is blown."

1906 International Pro. Hockey League

	GP	W	L	T	GF	GA	PTS
*Houghton-Portage Lakes	24	19	5	0	105	70	38
Michigan Soo Indians	24	18	6	0	126	57	36
Pittsburgh Pro HC	24	15	9	0	121	84	30
Calumet Miners	24	7	17	0	48	108	14
Canadian Soo	24	1	23	0	56	137	2

HOUGHTON 1906-07

Barney began the 1906-07 season, not with the Portage Lake team, but actually with the Winnipeg Strathconas of the Manitoba Professional League, who had outbid Houghton for his services. But after Barney played one (or possibly two) game(s) for the Strathconas (in which he scored one goal), Houghton came through with an offer that was acceptable to Holden, and he quickly rejoined his former Portage Lake teammates for the remainder of the season. The Strathconas only lasted one season and then folded.

The Portage Lakers were the favorite for the 1906-07 season, and appeared to be even stronger with the acquisition of "Tuff" Bellefeuille from the Kenora Thistles, and "Goldie" Cochrane (who was paid $600 just to complete the season) from an Ontario senior team. They knew they still needed Holden at coverpoint in order to retain the championship. Joining Holden, and the two new players, were Houghton veterans Fred Lake and Bruce Stuart; along with "Grindy" Forrester, Harry Bright, Fred Taylor, Dick Wilson, Cliff Hudson, Con Corbeau, "Doc" Gibson, and Harry Brown.

The Lakers went on to, once again, win the I.H.L. league pennant, which included beating Pittsburgh in a critical three-game series at the end of the season. Back in Houghton, a homecoming party awaited the conquering heroes just like the season before, and the entire town turned out again for the green and white parade through downtown Houghton, Michigan.

The Portage Lakers again sent word to the Stanley Cup Committee Board of Governors challenging Montreal to a championship. No dice. Nothing had changed as far as the Stanley Cup Board was concerned. No professional team would ever get a shot at the Cup.

After the celebration died down, the players quietly left Houghton, assuming they would return for the next year. Fred Taylor worked in a musical instrument factory, Goaltender Darcy Regan was a bartender, and Barney returned to the lumber mills of Winnipeg. Quite a few played lacrosse to keep in shape and earn a couple of bucks. The players had all planned to return to the IHL, if not to Houghton, for the 1907-08 season.

(Winnipeg newspaper February 1907)

HOUGHTON TAKES CHAMPIONSHIP

BARNEY HOLDEN'S TEAM AGAIN A WINNER

"The championship of the International Hockey League was practically decided this week. The honors go to Houghton for a second time in succession. In the three years of the International League's history, Houghton has had the championship twice and Calmut once."

The remainder of the article dealt with which teams were battling it out for second place. The standing of the clubs up until that point in the season was as follows:

Teams	W	L	Pct.
Houghton	14	7	.666
Pittsburg	12	11	.543
Canadian Soo	11	10	.523
Michigan Soo	8	12	.400
Calumet	8	14	.363

All Star Team

A follower of International League Hockey has chosen the following as an all star team:
Goal............Jack Winchester, Pittsburg
Point............Roy Brown, Canadian Soo
Coverpoint.....Barney Holden, Houghton

Rover...........Fred Taylor, Houghton
Centre..........Billy Taylor, Canadian Soo
Right wing.....Didier Petri, Michigan Soo
Left wing......Fred Lake, Houghton
Spares..........Laviolette, Michigan Soo
                    Campbell, Pittsburgh

In 1933, Winnipeg Tribune Magazine Sportswriter Norman J. Gillespie called the 1906 team one of the greatest hockey teams ever assembled. Gillespie stated that although the team consisted of all Canadians, "their skill and popularity helped introduce hockey into the United States." Once touted as "the greatest hockey aggregation ever gathered in the United States," the team included "Riley" Hern – Goalie, "Grindy" Forrester – Point, "Barney" Holden – Cover Point, Bruce Stuart (Captain) – Centre, "Bad" Joe Hall – Right Wing, Fred Lake – Left Wing, Fred "Cycone" Taylor and Harry Bright – Rovers, and Walter A. Forrest – Spare. Bruce, Stuart, Lake and Taylor were all from the Ottawa District of Manitoba. Hall was from Bandon, Manitoba; Bright and Holden were from Winnipeg.

Gillespie claimed that Barney was the greatest cover-point of all time, even greater than "Hod" Stuart. "He could make an individual rush that would make your hair stand on end, and he could pass and receive a pass with unerring accuracy," stated Gillespie.

> "He could shoot a puck with the accuracy of a rifle marksman...he could drive one in, ankle high, at the corner of the net. When the game was close...and his men were tired, he would stop a play, and stand at his position as cover point, and 'laze' a puck over the heads of all sundry that would find the goal."

Gillespie explained that the poor lighting in the old arenas made the puck difficult to see. "I have seen Barney score goal after goal by shooting a high one the length of the rink that would nestle in the net without the goalie ever knowing it was coming." By far, Gillespie's favorite story was about "blood on the ice," which occurred during the 1906-07 season in which Gillespie must have been working as a clubhouse boy. The Portage team was pitted against a professional team from Pittsburgh. Realizing Holden's propensity to knock in a critical goal or two, and more importantly, his reputation of eliminating opposing players, the Pittsburgh goons decided to get rid of him first. In the initial five minutes of the second half, a Pittsburgh player skated by Holden and intentionally gashed open his boot with his skate blade. Injured, but undaunted, Holden refused to leave the ice until the game was over. For 25 minutes he skated, leaving drops of blood all over the ice. "When he reached the dressing room," explained Gillespie, "this youth was there to wait on him, as usual, and drew off his shoe and poured blood out of the shoe. Could he take it?! A surgeon took seven stitches in his foot that night."

Unfortunately, what would have been the fourth season for the IHL would never happen…for a number of reasons. Even though the total Houghton payroll was only $5,000, it was too much for the owner. The players were demanding a larger salary, and the copper market was beginning to wane. Favoritism by hometown referees was becoming ridiculously blatant, and on-ice violence was getting worse. Pittsburgh had already decided to drop out of the IHPL before the next season, which would leave the league with no "big city" to count on for large receipts. Calumet, which had struggled to make any money at all, announced they would fold as well. Houghton was the final club to pull out. Attempts were made to attract clubs from Cleveland and Duluth, but to no avail. So on November 8, 1907, John McNamara, league secretary, announced there would be no more professional hockey in the Copper Country. But as luck would have it, by 1907 Canada finally decided to allow teams and players to join the professional ranks. The reason was simple…they had lost all their best players to the IHL! If you can't beat them, join them. So after three years the IHL folded. The first professional league in the world was no more. It was quickly replaced with an amateur league.

The success of the prior year had made all of the Portage Lakers very hot property, and each of them had no problem going back to Canada and hooking up with the new *Canadian* professional teams. But one thing had changed…these players demanded large salaries. Professional hockey was never the same. Holden mulled over several lucrative offers and then joined the Winnipeg Maple Leafs of the Manitoba Professional League.

By the time he left the Portage Lake team, Holden had played in 64 games for Houghton, more than any other Laker, with the exception of teammates Bruce Stuart (65), and Fred Lake (67). If you include the two games with the Winnipeg Strathconas, Barney actually played 66 games during the three-year season.

1907 International Pro. Hockey League

	GP	W	L	T	GF	GA	PTS
*Houghton-Portage Lakes	24	16	8	0	102	102	32
Canadian Soo	24	13	11	0	124	123	26
Pittsburgh Pro HC	25	12	12	1	94	82	25
Michigan Soo Indians	24	11	13	0	103	88	22
Calumet Wanderers	25	8	16	1	96	124	17

CHAPTER 3

//

WINNIPEG MAPLE LEAFS

"That was the toughest game I was ever in."

- Barney Holden, reminiscing in 1922 about a brutal game between the Maple Leafs and the Rowing Club in 1907

Barney stayed with the Maples Leafs for two seasons, which included a very short stint with the Montreal Wanderers who solicited his help in a failed attempt to win the Stanley Cup in 1908. Changing teams caused quit a stir in Winnipeg as the fans thought he was abandoning their team thus jeopardizing their own chances to win the cup. Holden first denied the rumor through his manager, but later felt obligated to explain his actions, and did so with the help of local sportswriters:

(Winnipeg Newspaper 1907)

IS HOLDEN GOING EAST?

"Rumor was current last night that Barney Holden, the dashing cover point and captain of the Maple Leaf hockey team, had closed negotiations with the Montreal Wanderers and would go east next week to finish out the season with the Stanley Cup holders as cover point. It was stated that he wired his acceptance to Art Ross, the Wanderer captain, last night. It is known that Barney has had many tempting inducements held out to him to join various eastern teams, but Manager Lee last night emphatically denied that Holden would leave. He stated that Holden had turned down the offers, and would continue to hold down the cover position for the local team and would, more than that, lead them east after the Stanley Cup this spring."

"Considerable talk has been recently floating around to the effect that Barney Holden, the sturdy cover point of the Maple Leafs, intended going East to finish out the season with the Montreal Wanderers, holders of the Stanley Cup."

The writer was able to confirm that the rumors were true; Barney had accepted an offer to leave the Maple Leafs and join the Montreal Wanderers. However, the sports writer was able to set the record straight:

"...this chatter, if it had gone very much farther, would have seriously injured Holden in the eyes of the Winnipeg sporting public, and would have been unjust at the same time. The true spirit of sportsmanship pervades greatly in the West, but Holden would never have been forgiven if he had deserted the Maple Leafs...at a time when they needed his services more than any other part of the season...in the thick of the fight for the Manitoba championship...but in justice to him, from the start he did not entertain the remotest idea of leaving the Leafs, notwithstanding the dispatch from Montreal to the effect that he would join the Wanderers immediately. Barney did make arrangements with the Wanderers to play for them, but it was only on the understanding that he would not leave the Leafs until they had been put out of the running for the championship."

The writer pointed out this was quite a different scenario than abandoning one's team when they needed you the most.

"Holden is to be commended, as it is understood that the offer made him was considerably in excess of the salary he is drawing as a Maple Leaf." This news was welcomed by the Winnipeg fans who viewed Holden as, "the king of the Western cover points."

This was such a newsworthy event at the time, that it would be mentioned years later in a Winnipeg Province sports column entitled, *Twenty Years Ago in Sport*, in which it stated, "Barney Holden of Winnipeg Maple Leafs joins Montreal Wanderers."

One of the more memorable games that Barney recalled later from his years with the Maple Leafs involved a dispute between the Winnipeg Maple Leafs and the Rowing Club. The Rowing Club had been the amateur champions, and both teams thought they should be admitted into the "professional circuit"…but there was only room for one. So it was decided that the teams would play one another, and the winner would get the berth. It's difficult to say who threw the first punch, or at what point the game escalated into an all out war, but the encounter erupted into a dreadful confrontation that Barney later described as "the roughest game he was ever in." The Maple Leafs apparently had gained an edge over the Rowing Club during the melee. Perhaps they wanted it more. Finally, the game became too grueling for the Rowing Club who simply threw up their hands and skated off the ice. The Maple Leafs were awarded the victory, and later the league title, and then challenged the Montreal Wanderers for the Stanley Cup. However, the Leafs failed in the attempt.

1907/08 - MANITOBA PROFESSIONAL HOCKEY LEAGUE

Compiled by *www.puckerings.com* from the Manitoba Free Press. Assists and minutes played are unofficial - assigned based on game summaries.

Results	GP	W	L	T	GF	GA	PCT
Winnipeg Maple Leafs	17	1	16	0	111	89	.647
Portage Plains Cities	15	8	7	0	76	72	.533
Winnipeg Strathconas	16	6	10	0	106	114	.375
Brandon Wheat Cities	1	0	1	0	0	4	.000
Kenora Thistles	1	0	1	0	1	15	.000

Brandon and Kenora folded - results not counted in official standings

Winnipeg Maple Leafs

	POS	GP	G	A	TP	P	IMMIN
Darcy Regan	G	16	0	0	0	0	960
Lorne Campbell	C/R	16	32	4	36	50	953
"Barney" Holden	CP	16	4	3	7	24	936
Billy "Cotton-Top" Keane	R	15	21	6	27	18	824
Harry Kennedy	RW	13	23	6	29	15	765
"Grindy" Forrester	P	11	2	1	3	9	651
Jim Jackson	LW	10	10	4	14	12	588
Billy Field #	LW	6	3	2	5	3	357
Tommy Dunderdale	P	4	1	1	2	3	237
Lorne Hannay	P	2	1	0	1	0	120
Hamby Shore*	C	1	4	0	4	0	60
Frank Switzer*	RW	1	1	0	1	0	60
Jack Winchester*	G	1	0	0	0	0	60
Fred Lake*	LW	1	0	3	3	3	57
		17	105	30	135	137	1020

	GP	MIN	GA	GAA
Jack Winchester*	1	60	3	3.00
Darcy Regan	16	960	86	5.38
	17	1020	89	5.24

Jumped to the Strathconas from Maple Leafs for second half of season.

* *Jumped from the Strathconas to Maple Leafs for second half of season.*

CHAPTER 4

//

MONTREAL SHAMROCKS

"Barney Holden is showing eastern hockey critics that he can play hockey..."

- Ottawa Free Press, 1909

In 1909, Holden accepted an offer from the Montreal Shamrocks for $800 per season, and he decided to move east to give them a taste of tough Western-style hockey.

The Shamrocks hockey team grew out of the Shamrocks Lacrosse team, world champions at the Chicago World's Fair in 1893. It was an era of religious prejudice and Catholics did not play on the wasp-dominated teams of the Amateur Hockey Association (AHA). The Shamrocks hockey team was started with support from Pastor John Quinlivan of St. Patrick's Church (now basilica). The Shamrocks joined the AHA in 1895 and the newly-formed Canadian Amateur Hockey League in 1898. The Shamrocks had won the Stanley Cup in 1899 and 1900. As hockey moved into the 20th century the club was looking for yet another championship.

SHAMROCKS CAME NEAR UNLOADING THE SEASON'S SURPRISE ON OTTAWA

───────────

With Two Home-Brew Intermediates on the Team, They Had Ottawa Badly Up in the Air Till the Last Ten Minutes, When Champs. Settled Down and Won 9-6

───────────

This Montreal newspaper article, which appeared in the winter of 1908, explained how the Montreal Shamrocks nearly upset the current champions even when the Shamrocks added three "minor league" players to fill out the roster. The Irish had them on the run for awhile, but then Ottawa came on strong at the end and the Shamrocks "faded, fairly wilted, like fresh cut flowers put out in the strong sun," according to the local paper. Despite the loss, the sportswriter pointed out Holden's play during the game: "Barney Holden, who played a magnificent game throughout, burst through the whole Ottawa defence and started the ball rolling. Joe Hall and Tommie (sic) Dunderdale followed up with good work, and to their surprise Ottawa found themselves one goal behind at half time." Going into the second half the Shamrocks scored again and led the champions 5-3. Ottawa then scored quickly, followed by the Shamrocks when, "…Barney Holden with another fine individual effort scored again and things were looking good for Shamrocks…" During the game Tommy Dunderdale of the Shamrocks took a puck in the mouth, as did Fred Lake and "Small" of Ottawa. The article concluded by stating, "Barney Holden is playing one of the cleanest defence games in the hockey series."

The Shams bounced back in their next game against All-Montreal with vigor:

"MONTREAL, Jan. 4 --- The Shamrocks tonight showed a return to their old form and in the best exhibition of hockey this season tonight defeated the All-Montreal team in the Canadian association game by 6-3. The Shamrocks showed wonderful improvement over their style in last Saturday's game against Quebec, and held All-Montreal in check from start to finish. They scored three goals in the first half, holding All-Montreal from (scoring) at all. In the second half, with Holden who had played a star game, on the fence for twenty minutes, they showed real strength by holding All-Montreal to an even division of goals of three each. Ten minutes after the opening of the second half, with the score 5-1,

Holden was hurt, and after that the Shamrocks were more on the defensive with the result that each side scored two goals. The play through out was brilliant, the extreme cold making the ice very fast, and the fifteen hundred people who attended the game were kept in a continual state of enthusiasm until the final whistle."

The line-up:

All-Montreal	Position	Shamrocks
Moran	goal	Baker
Ross	point	Hill
Pvey	cover	Holden
Kane	rover	Dunderdale
Norman	centre	Smith
Liffeton	right wing	Mulcaier
Marks	left wing	Bellamy

Over the next several years, many of the former Houghton players, as well as International Hockey League players from the other teams, would cross paths as team mates and opponents. Old friendships could be quickly forgotten in the heat of battle, as was the case in a Renfrew / Shamrock game. This game was never actually completed due to a combination of a flooded rink and a surplus of bad tempers. The unusually warm weather caused the ice to turn to mush, which caused the players to slog around in the slush and tumble into pools of water. Unfortunately, warm weather was always an issue the early hockey players had to deal with. Anyway, by the second half, tempers flared and bedlam ensued when Barney, fed up what he perceived to be Fred Taylor's plethora of cheap shots, lost his cool and took a swing at Fred's head with his stick. Luckily, Fred ducked, or the results could have been very serious. Taylor quickly retaliated by raising his stick and catching Barney under the nose, and the blood started to flow. Then all hell broke loose as players attacked each other in what the newspaper reported as a tremendous mass of "slashing and swiping."

BARNEY HOLDEN PLAYED STAR GAME

But Shamrocks Blew Up at Finish Permitting Ottawas to Win Out

---

"Montreal, Feb.23, 1908 – The Shamrocks came near unloading the surprise of the hockey season tonight, when up to the last ten minutes of their game with the champion Ottawas they were in the lead."

"Easily the feature of the Shamrock play throughout was the performance of Barney Holden, the former Winnipegger, now playing coverpoint for the Shamrock team. The defence of the Irish seven has weakened considerably since Winchester deserted and Forrester was flagged. On Holden fell the brunt of the work and he did it all. When he was not checking the rushes of the Ottawas he was taking a hand in the attack. Two of the Shamrock goals were scored entirely on his individual efforts, while two others of the remaining four originated with brilliant runs up the ice. Holden gained many admirers since he started the season here in Montreal. The general opinion of his work is that on a classy team he would rank as one of the greatest defence players in the game."

The article explained that while Joe Hall and Tommy Dunderdale did good work that night, they weren't having their usual game. "Dunderdale got a nasty crack in the mouth from a rising puck early in the game and though he went right on with the game, the injury seemed to slow him up considerably." Even in those days, a good pop in the chops could make you go soft. The next night the Shamrocks were to play Haileybury. The local Montreal newspaper, in an effort to boost attendance, listed a string of jumbled hockey-related items in their "Sporting Notes" column:

- "Haileybury vs. Shams to-night. Come and see J. Hall, the Wild Man of the West."
- "With Bellamy playing at point for the Shams, look out for spectacular runs up the ice. He can go like a streak."
- "Under the circumstance the only thing for the league officials to do is to order that Shamrock-Renfrew game to be played over, with a special request to J. Hall to cut out the Jim Jeffries doings" *(Jim Jeffries was the heavyweight boxing champion from 1899 to 1905).*
- "Another chance to-night to see P. (Paddy) Moran, the demon goalkeeper."
- "The uniforms worn by some of the pro. teams this year are a fright. It's a crime to make our fair athletes appear in public in such a riot of color."
- "After this officials should watch Mr. F. (Frank) Patrick a little closer. He played the kind of game Saturday that should have made him stay in the penalty coop longer than he was."
- "It is a pleasure to see a hockey game in the Arena, after viewing the sport in some of the smoke-laden barns in the rest of the circuit."

As a side note, while some things in hockey constantly evolved, the need to fill the seats with cash-paying patrons never did. Hence the Madison Avenue attempt at luring the crowd above with the reference to Bellamy, Patrick, and Moran. Recently, in the Portland (Oregon) newspaper, the Oregonian, the Portland Winter Hawks, a junior league professional team, tempted the sports fan with the following advertisement regarding their upcoming game against Kootenay, British Columbia, Canada:

"**Robin Big Snake**, 6' 0", 212 lbs – 129 Penalty Minutes. Yes, that's his real name and he's just as tough as it sounds. Come watch Big Snake and your Winter Hawks Friday night."

Some things never change, but that fact of the matter is that you have to bring in the gate receipts for any professional sport to thrive. Anyway, back to Holden…

Word of Holden's performance on the Shamrock team was always relayed back to the Winnipeg papers so they could keep track of their hometown boy.

(Ottawa Free Press, 1908)

WINNIPEG PLAYER HIGHLY COMMENDED

Barney Holden's Defence Was Compared To That Of Hod Stuart

"The Montreal Gazette has the following to say of the Winnipeg team that figured in the game with All-Montreal last week: 'A feature of the game was the fine play of Barney Holden, the Shamrocks cover point. In the first half he gave a display of defence work that recalled Hod Stuart at his best. He showed splendid judgment breaking up rushes and time and again carried the disc to the other end of the rink, showing the same good judgment and unselfishness that used to mark the play of Stuart.' The Ottawa Free Press also lauded Barney as follows: 'Barney Holden is showing eastern hockey critics that he can play hockey…Two years ago, when Winnipeg Maples Leafs were coming east for the Stanley Cup, both Wanderers and Ottawa made frenzied efforts to get the big fellow, but he turned down some hefty monetary offers. He played fine hockey for Portage the year Bruce Stuart was running the team.'"

The following is one of the more interesting games played by the Montreal Shamrocks during the 1908 season. Initially reported as a rather dull game, it was anything but.

SHAMROCKS, 8 TO 3

Seven Representing Irishmen Easily Defeated Canadiens at Arena Last Night

POOR EXHIBITION OF HOCKEY

Play livened Up After Dull First Half, but Both Teams Showed Indifferent Form

According to the author of this newspaper article, this was a very boring game between the Shamrocks and Canadiens, especially to the "upwards of 2,000 spectators who turned out in hope of a fast, exciting clash between the Irish and the French." But perhaps that wasn't exactly true, as the remainder of the story seemed to indicate that, while not a great display of hockey skills, it was more like a *donnybrook* on ice, which hockey crowds usually find rather exciting.

The first half was sluggish with both teams having trouble getting off the mark. Even though the Shamrocks scored three times in the first half, it must have looked laborious and disorganized. Barney Holden was responsible for the first goal. "He had just served a penalty, and, carrying the disc down the ice, shot around Laviolette. Groulx stopped (the puck), but fell, and Boulton poked the disc in." After that goal, Bernier of the Canadians went after Holden giving him brutal cross-check to the head. Holden was dazed, but unfettered, and Bernier was sent to the box.   Later, one of the Shamrocks delivered retribution by skating by and cracking Bernier over the eye with his stick. Then the Canadians went after Holden again: "The worst foul occurred in the second half…for hooking Holden viciously." Tommy Dunderdale and Decarie of the Canadiens collided later in the game, forcing Dunderdale to take a short break off the ice to recover. It was interesting to note that Shamrock goalie, Winchester, was sent off the ice for two minutes "for dropping to his knees in making a stop." In those days the goalie had to stay on his feet when blocking the puck.

"There was a succession of minor accidents throughout the match. Players were continually bumping into one another in the scrambly hockey and some received nasty blows." Even the two referees, Bowie and Melville, were slammed to the ice a few times. "Newsy" Lalonde was too ill to play in this particular game; the reporter stating that he feared *Newsy* had come down with Typhoid Fever! Despite both squads showing a lack of team play that, "was painful at times," the reporter praised Holden's performance. "In the disorganized hockey, Holden's work stood out favorably. The Shamrocks cover played his usual steady game; rushed well, and good support would have brought Shamrock's tally to larger figures."   Holden scored with five minutes remaining "after a clever run" and "Bad" Joe Hall scored in the last two minutes having received a pass from Holden. Hall, who had behaved "exemplary" all game, must have committed some sort of infraction as he was booted from the game with less than two minutes to go.

(January 1, 1909)

SHAMROCKS BEAT
ALL-MONTREAL, 6-3

Led 3 to 0 in First Half and Held the Game
Safe at All Stages

Winnipeg Trio Showed Good Form, Play of Holden, Until
Injured, Being a Feature

"In the best exhibition of hockey so far this season, Shamrocks made a recovery from the poor form shown against Quebec on New Year's Day, defeating All-Montreal in a Canadian Association game at the Arena last night by a score of 6 goals to 3."

The Shamrocks controlled the entire game. Ten minutes into the second half, Holden, "who had been playing star hockey" in the first half, went down with a puck to the groin and did not return. Ouch. An All-Montreal player was then taken off the ice to even out the teams. Hockey had progressed at least to the point where the teams would match each other in regards to the number of players.

"Holden's strength to Shamrocks had been such during the previous forty minutes that his loss weakened Shamrocks to an extent that gave All-Montreal a very fair chance to even it up." However, with the score already 5 to 3, All-Montreal could not catch-up.

At the opening of the second half, "Rocket" Power of the Canadiens tossed out a half-dozen lemons in the direction of Shamrock goalie, Paddy Moran. Like many of the league's players, they were all friends, having played together on different teams. So this was Power's way to tell his old friend what he though of his goal-tending ability. This game was unusually cold, and the ice was "too keen for some of the player's skates and there were many tumbles." One of the All-Montreal players even suffered a "left frozen foot."

> "A feature of the game was the fine play of Barney
> Holden, the Shamrock cover point. In the first half
> he gave a display of defence work that recalled Hod
> Stuart at his best. He showed splendid judgement in
> breaking up rushes and time and again carried the
> disc to the other end of the rink, showing the same
> good judgement and unselfishness that used to mark
> the play of Stuart."

Of all of the many descriptions of hockey games that were
researched for this book, this one by far exceeds the others for
muddled verbiage coupled with nonsensical phrases. However,
reading the story does get your pulse racing, even if the writing
is silly. Perhaps the sportswriter was actually a frustrated poet
or stage actor, as each paragraph reads like a stanza from one
of Shakespeare's soliloquies. One can almost image the writer
standing in knee-highs, holding Yorick's skull in his outstretched
hand, with his press card tucked behind his ear; "I knew him,
Horatio; a fellow of infinite jest…" It was often times difficult
to follow the flow of the game as one sifted through all of the
flowery rhetoric. He even appeared to invent words. The sports
writing of the Victorian era was often absurd, but it wasn't
usually this bad. The writer launched his article by attempting to
set the stage for the reader:

> "And so, when, at the call of the whistle, fourteen
> stalwart young fellows rushed upon the ice, every
> creature fixed himself in his seat with a longing, yet
> a fearful expectancy. Was there anything wrong? Ah,
> it was the ice. Soft and spongy, retarding the pace
> and adding lead to the puck."

The Shamrocks apparently dominated the game, but had
troubling finding the goal due to the tough Haileybury defense.
The writer pointed out the style of play by Bellamey of the
Shamrocks and calling his style…

> "...valencieness (sic) lace of hockey. It gives ornateness (sic) to the ordinary. It uplifts the spirits. It makes femininity gasp with joy and terror. As the fat boy in Dickens delighted to 'freeze yer blood,' so Bellamy and Art Ross delight to thrill the crowd, which...when that is productive of immediate results, loves the dainty suggestion of embroidery, so dear to the common heart."

At nearly the end of the first half, the writer reflected on the play thus far: "And so Bellamy and Holden and Dunderdale and Smith, put forth a supreme effort, and the crowd cried game again." Shot after shot failed to find the Haileybury net, and then the tide turned, and Shamrock goalie, Paddy Moran was now on the hot-seat. A goalie still could not lie on the ice to block the puck, but if you were clever enough to make it look like an accident, that was a different story. And that's exactly what Moran did.

> "Moran flings himself on the ice. There is a scrimmage. A man biffing and slapping and poking for the puck, which is within an inch of the visitor's goals a dozen times. And now the crowd is passing through those emotional storms which will leave it limp on the morrow. It is standing up yelling, screaming encouragement to the Shamrocks in full throated chorus. Now Bellamy and Holden surpassed themselves. And now Ross and Ronan, Dey and Smith, wrought wonders. Team play, brilliant bits of individual play, deft passing – the elusive Holden, the giant frame of Bellamy, as light, too, as thistledown as one might say; the clever stopping at both ends; the splendid defence of the Shamrocks; the quick clearing of the visitors, with cheers and cries to punctuate the play – there was all this and more."

The Shamrocks apparently scored, and were now leading, 2-1, with five minutes left in the game. "And now the crowd rose, and remained standing; and the women went through those poignant experiences which give life its vividity; and the poorest sport in the place was willing to bet his last ten cent piece on the issue of a titanic contest." In the final seconds of the game, Halibury got tough and scored, once again tying the game,

2-2. "This only served to increase the poignancy of interest," claimed the writer. The match then went into overtime, and within thirty seconds the Shamrocks scored again and won the match, "which was a delight to witness," and, "was marking by close and brilliant play on both sides." Yet despite its wacky descriptions, the article wasn't without its charm.

Some times the players had to deal with weather conditions that would certainly never occur in present day games. The following is an interesting match-up that occurred during a warm weather trend. Incidentally, this article appears to have been written by the same poetic sportswriter as before. Interestingly enough, he starts out writing in his usual flamboyant style, but halfway through the article he switches to more blow-by-blow reporting. Perhaps his well of poetic inspiration ran dry.

TROUBLE AT RENFREW SHAMROCK MATCH

"Rivers, lakes, inland oceans. A puck that got lost; that had to be fished for; that, instead of landing in St. Henry, refused to budge an inch; that made ripples on the water; that stopped dead when it should have been mobile and swift as lightning. And, in spite of the unprecedented and depressing conditions – hockey, brilliant hockey – 'dandy hockey,' as the cynic called it."

For the first time, the arena had been filled with cheering fans, and perhaps the warmth of all those bodies, coupled with warmer than usual conditions, caused the ice to melt in spots. The crowd seemed to enjoy the spectacle all the more as evidenced by the prosaic sportswriter:

> "It stood up on its hind legs. It yelled and cheered; it waved its hat; it roared encouragement or shrieked its condemnation. As the men splashed through the water, it urged them on."

Occasionally play would be stopped so the attendants could slide onto the ice and scoop up buckets of water. But to no avail. The game began with the Shamrocks defending their goal at the north end as Gordon of the Renfrew team took the puck up the ice. However, he was unable to pass Holden who stole the puck and passed up to one of the Shamrock forwards. A few minutes later Fred Taylor had the puck for Refrew but was completely lifted off his feet by a blow from Bellamy of the Shamrocks. By half-time the Shamrocks were leading, 1-0.

The players were exhausting themselves skating in molasses-like conditions, and smacking the puck with all their might, only to have it travel a few yards and stop dead in a pool of slush. The best thing to do was for the defenders to try to lift the puck into the air and down the ice. So when not ducking flying pucks, the players just stood there, dripping wet, trying to figure out how to best play in such conditions, and then watched their teammates as they splashed and sprayed in pools of ice water. Some would get up a head of steam and appear to cruise down the ice, then skate right into a stagnant pool of slush and end up doing a face-plant and sliding on their bellies. Players even had trouble seeing the puck as slush was constantly being splashed in their eyes. Canceling the game wasn't an option in those days...players just had to make the best of it. It was a melee. Water splashed and tempers flared. Even the "judge of play" was mistakenly attacked in a blind rage by "Bad" Joe Hall of the Shamrocks. This occurred because all through out the game Frank Patrick would skate by and tap Joe Hall on the head with his stick. Hockey historians claim that Patrick was the only player not intimidated by Hall, and that was certainly evident in this particular game. Finally when Patrick cut Hall's eye, Patrick was sent to the penalty box. But later, when Patrick was back in the game, and Hall was skating towards the Refrew goal, Patrick knew he was playing with fire, but he once again struck Hall on the head. This time Hall skated to a halt, whipped around and punched Patrick in the face, lacerating Patrick's cheek and sending him reeling. The two men went at each other, falling to the ice, and in the scuffle Hall was cut over the eye a second time by Patrick's stick. Judge of Play, Rod Kennedy, tried to pull the two apart but was attacked by Hall who was blinded by the blood in his eyes and mistook him for one of the Renfrew players who were now coming to the aid of Patrick. Lester Patrick, Frank's brother, tried to intervene, but was intercepted by Smith of the Shamrocks who pinned Lester Patrick against the fence with his stick. When the melee finally ended, Hall was tossed from the game, but Patrick was only given a three-minute penalty, even though it was his second infraction. Referee Thomas Hodge disagreed with Kennedy and said Hall should return, claiming the attack on Kennedy as unintentional. While the referees argued with each other, and with the game still tied, the Shamrocks skated out onto the ice to show their willingness to play. The officials then decided Hall would return to the ice. It was at that point the Renfrew team refused to play, citing the personal conflict between Patrick and Hall, the striking of the official, and the condition of the ice. However, the main reason was because of Hall. If he was allowed back on the ice, Renfrew would not play, plain and simple. So the game remained a 1-1 tie, much to the dismay of the fans.

"It was a disappointed crowd that jammed, packed, choked the street cars," wrote the sportswriter. It should be noted that only Hall and Frank Patrick scored in that game. But the crowd continued to encourage their local heroes, nonetheless. The writer had another beauty of a comparison regarding the initial "genteel crowd" who came to life as rink conditions deteriorated and play became very intense: "…as a famous writer has said

– 'Judy O'Grady and the Captain's lady are sisters under the skin,' and, in the provocative moment, it is the dainty creature who splits her gloves in her demonstrations of feeling."

The author ended the article with the following comments on a few of the players:

"For there were Holden and Dunderdale ever on the alert, quick, resolute; and Bellamy, the strong and capable; and Smith and Hall, offering beautiful team play... Taylor was there in all his speed and glory, with his old tricks, his speed, his elusiveness."

(1908)

WANDERER-SHAMROCK MATCH WAS FAST EXHIBITION ALTHOUGH SCORE ONE-SIDED

First Part of First Half Shamrocks More Than Held Their Own

Efforts Faded in the Second as Score Mounted Up Against Them

The writer of this article explained that despite the 10-1 victory for the Montreal Wanderers over the Shamrocks, the Shams actually performed quite well in the beginning, slamming shot after shot at the Wanderer goal, with one shot finding the back of the net. Later, however, the Shams "blew up" and the Wanderer goals began to rack up. The writer pointed out that the one bright spot on the Shamrocks team was the play of Barney Holden:

"Barney Holden was the Shamrock Star. Barney played the best game he has ever played in the East.

Consistent at all times and clever to a degree that by blocking…he robbed opposing players of the puck… The support he got was, however, insufficient…"

After the writer droned on about how the Shamrocks had screwed up the game, he came back to Barney again.

"It remained for Holden to start the scoring. Just over eleven minutes from the start he burst down the ice with Bellamy along side and a pass and re-pass enabled him to get Shamrock's single tally from close in."

The Teams:

Wanderers		Shamrocks
Hern	Goal	Winchester
Marshall	Point	Forrester
Johnson	Coverpoint	Holden
Glass	Rover	Dunderdale
Russell	Centre	Smith
Gardener	L. Wing	Bellamy
Hyland	R. Wing	Hall

One of the last descriptions of Holden's play with the Shamrocks really summed up his talent: "Holden was the darling of the crowd. Bright he was, too, and swift as the ice would let him. He was great in dashes, in cutting out the puck in taking long odds." The Montreal Shamrocks club folded after the 1909-10 season and Holden and "Bad" Joe Hall then jumped to the Quebec Bulldogs of the National Hockey Association (the precursor to the NHL) for $900 each for the season. This was the first professional season for Quebec.

1908/09 - MANITOBA PROFESSIONAL HOCKEY LEAGUE

Winnipeg Maple Leafs

	POS	GP	G	A	TP	PIM	MIN
Jack Winchester	G	9	0	0	0	0	43
"Barney" Holden	P	9	3	4	7	9	534
"Grindy" Forrester	CP	8	7	4	11	6	477
John Jackson	RW	8	8	2	10	9	439
Harry Nesbitt	C	9	18	2	20	3	418
Jim Jackson	LW	7	11	5	16	12	411
Georges "Kid" Poulin	R/RW	7	12	4	16	18	394
Billy "Cotton-Top" Keane	R	5	8	2	10	9	252
"Bad" Joe Hall	RW	2	2	1	3	0	84
Hugh Ross	R/C	2	2	1	3	6	85

	GP	MIN	GA	GAA		
Jack Winchester	9	543	68	7.51		
	9	71	25	96	72	543

Results	GP	W	L	T	GF	GA	PCT
Winnipeg Shamrocks	9	5	4	0	69	64	.556
Winnipeg Maple Leafs	9	5	4	0	72	68	.556
Winnipeg Winnipegs	2	0	2	0	13	22	.000

Compiled by *www.puckerings.com* from the Manitoba Free Press. Assists and minutes played are unofficial - assigned based on game summaries.

1909 - 10 FINAL STANDINGS

	GP	W	L	T	PTS	GF	GA
Montreal Wanderers	12	11	1	0	22	91	41
Ottawa Senators	12	9	3	0	18	89	66
Renfrew Cream.Kings	12	8	3	1	17	96	54
Cobalt Silver Kings	12	4	8	0	8	79	104
Haileybury Hockey Club	12	4	8	0	8	77	83
Montreal Shamrocks	12	3	8	1	7	52	95
Montreal Canadiens	12	2	10	0	4	59	104

CHAPTER 5

QUEBEC BULLDOGS

"Holden, though, now rated as a veteran, is a good
defence man…He gets down the ice well and it is
pretty hard work to get by him. Quebec was without
a point man and all the defence work fell on Holden's
shoulder."

- Quebec Newspaper account of a game in 1910

Holden was the first to join the Bulldogs and don the Quebec
sweater with large blue "Q" trimmed in white. Tommy Dunderdale
and Eddie Oatman, his Montreal Shamrocks teammates, were fed
up with the sport for various reasons and had considered quitting
the game entirely. Holden wired them from Quebec and insisted
they not give up on professional hockey. His wire also included
offers to come join him and play for Quebec, which they did. It
was at Quebec that both Oatman and Dunderdale would prove
themselves to be high caliber players and their careers would
eventually land both of them in the Hall of Fame.

Officially known as "Athletics," the Bulldogs roots went
back to 1888 in the Amateur Hockey Association. The name
came about when a reporter referred to their tenacious style
of play. The name seemed popular with media and fans so the
team adopted a Bulldog mascot. However officially their name
remained Athletics.1910 was also the year that the NHA decided
to change from two 30-minute halves to three 20-minute periods.
They also decided to eliminate the "rover" position and go to six
men per side.

The CAHL would be come the ECAHA as the desire to
become a professional league overwhelmed Amateur hockey
leading to the formation of the Canadian Hockey Association in

1909, in which the Quebec Bulldogs were a founding member. However, after just one month the CHA merged into the more powerful National Hockey Association. The Bulldogs were not sure they wanted to join, so they sat out the rest of the season. By the time Holden, Oatman, and Dunderdale joined Quebec in 1910, Quebec was ready to become part of the NHA.

(Quebec Newspaper, December 1910)

QUEBEC DOWNED THE RENFREW TEAM

Beat Millionaires 3 to 2 in First Senior Hockey Match

"Quebec's reappearance in Canada's big league of professional hockey clubs was marked by victory in their first league match of the season with Renfrew at the Quebec Rink last night which they clinched by a margin of 3 goals to 2."

Two-thousand fans watched "the local classy seven" beat the visiting Millionaires. The weather conditions were not favorable and the heat from the packed house began to melt the ice making the going somewhat sluggish. Interestingly enough, Millionaire star, Fred "Cyclone" Taylor, was apparently covered so closely by the Bulldogs that he was virtually ineffective. That didn't happen to "Cyc" very often. The report stated there were no standouts on the Bulldog team as everyone performed admirably:

"Paddy Moran, in goals, stopped shots from near and far proving that he has not lost any of his cleverness, while Barney Holden, as foxsy (sic) as any of the young fellows, who would find it difficult to teach the veteran anything on the finer points of the game. Barney was a surprise to all, as he had very little practice so far this season, arriving here at the latter part of last week. His blocking and rushes were the features."

The writer chose to mention a subject that had been gaining more attention in the professional leagues. Smoking.

"The rink was a cloud of smoke which made it difficult for the spectators to distinguish the players. It was also very trying on the teams who had to battle on such a soft sheet (of ice). It is regrettable that stricter measures are not enforced by the rink authorities to prohibit this. It is true that the press men did join in making the fog, but they abstained until all hands seemed to be puffing the weed."

The team line-ups were as follows:

QUEBEC: Paddy Moran, Joe Power, Barney Holden, Ken Mallen, Eddie Oatman, Joe Malone, J. McDonald.
RENFREW: S. Cleghorn, R. Smith, O. Cleghorn, Rowe, Fred Taylor, McNamara, Lindsay.

(Quebec Newspaper, January 1910)

OTTAWA AND QUEBEC PLAYED 3 MEN ASIDE FOR FOUR MINUTES OF THE LAST HALF

Hilarious Contest at Arena Had 5,000 People in an Uproar

Joe Hall Injured Shoulder in Accident and is Out of Game Score 13-5.

"Five thousand spectators who attended the Ottawa-
Quebec game at the Arena Saturday night witnessed
the unique spectacle of three men aside striving to
score on the other's goal for four minutes of the last
period."

Apparently the teams were reduced to three per side due to a
rash of penalties, and the other side was forced to reduce players
as well, per league rules. Bruce Ridpath of Ottawa scored twice
during this time in what was described as a "burlesque" where
the remnants of both teams were desperately trying to block
their nets. After about four minutes the players streamed out of
the penalty boxes and back onto the ice, bringing both teams up
to normal strength. "Bad" Joe Hall had just joined the Quebec
Bulldogs a few days earlier, and the team had high hopes that
he would help them defeat Ottawa. Hall was a real draw for any
team. Much like watching a train wreck, the audience came to
see Hall clobber someone. When he did throw a few checks, the
crowd would roar all the way from the expensive seats to the
"quarter dollar boys in the north end."   In the middle of
the second period, however, after a lackluster performance in
which Hall was moved from center to point, he attempted to
body check Jack Darragh of the Ottawa team near the boards.
Both men were traveling a full speed when Hall tripped over
Darragh's skate and Joe's head and shoulder crashed into the
board "with a resounding crack." Hall got up, but was noticeably
dazed, and "wandered aimlessly about the ice with his arm
hanging limp." The referee thought he was "shamming" and
did not stop the game. During this time Ottawa scored again.
Finally the referee realized Hall wasn't faking and he stopped
the game so Joe could leave the ice. It turned out that Hall had
dislocated his shoulder and he was taken to St. Luke's Hospital
for treatment. Quebec had no further substitutes, so both teams
had to play with six a side. Scoring continued on both sides
including a combination by Holden and Mallen for Quebec's
fifth goal.

As if the game wasn't strange enough, Barney ended up losing a suspender button on his trousers while he was taking the puck down the ice. Holding his pants with one hand, and navigating the puck with the other, he desperately looked for someone to pass to before the game was finally stopped so Barney could "readjust his garmet." Apparently the incident didn't go unnoticed. "The whole rink was hep to the situation and it was productive of one of the numerous laughs of the night," wrote the reporter the next day. The spectators must have found it ironic that Holden was "holden" up his pants. Despite the loss to Ottawa, the reporter pointed out the excellent defense work of Holden and Jackey McDonald:

> "...Jackey McDonald on the line and Barney Holden on the defence were easily the choice. McDonald always has been a clever wing, able to carry the puck and can shoot well. Holden, though, now rated as a veteran, is a good defence man and showed to advantage Saturday. He gets down the ice well and it is pretty hard work to get by him. Quebec was without a point man and all the defence work fell on Holden's shoulder."

This game was also one of the first in which "no smoking" signs were hung in the Ottawa arena. The players said it helped their breathing considerably. All of the spectators complied, with the exception of the "rush seat crowd."

As a note, by 1910 the NHA still played seven-man hockey using a rover along with the other "traditional" six positions. The defensemen were called "point men" and one played point or "defensive defenseman" while the other played "counterpoint" (also know as "cover-point") and was an "offensive defenseman." The later was always Barney's position, which is why he could slip in a goal now and then, but that wasn't what he was hired to do. He was hired to stop the other team from scoring, as evidenced below. The NHA did change from two 30-

minute halves to three 20-minute periods. That remains to this day.

(Quebec Newspaper, January 1911)

CANADIEN DEFEATED QUEBEC, BUT ONLY AFTER VISITORS HAD THEM BADLY SCARED

George Kennedy's Speed Boys Were Not Playing at the Top of Their Form, and the Game was Nearly Over When LaLonde Notched the Winning Goal

"It was a scant margin that Canadiens had to the good when the last signal was tapped out at the Arena on Saturday night and the speedy Frenchman led Quebec at the finish by three goals to two." The reporter when on to state that he felt this game harked back to the *old* days:

> "It was real hockey. Real hockey! It was a close approach to the old days as when there were four forwards working together. They called it 'combination' then. It is so seldom seen now that it is nameless. To Quebec must be given full credit for giving an exhibition of real combination, and it worked so well that the other fellows used it, too."

Apparently Quebec beat the Canadiens in combination play, but "the Franco-Hibernian crew had the speed to check back and that quality was the factor that brought the victory to them." The article pointed out the excellent goal-tending by Paddy Moran, who blocked a number of "herculean" shots from Didier Pitre of the Canadiens, as well as the scoring ability of "Newsey" Lalonde who slipped in the winning goal. Tommy Dunderdale and Joe Malone performed well against the Canadiens' "speedy checks," but both were later taken out of the game, "apparently suffering from the effects of heavy slams to the ice." The Quebec defence outshone the Canadiens, "and Barney Holden was the star performer of the defence men, his play standing out."

(Quebec Newspaper, January 1911)

QUEBEC WON FROM CANADIEN

Gave the Speedy Septette One of the Hardest Runs of Season

"Quebec seems to have struck its gait at last, and last night's victory will not be the only one chalked up to its credit during the closing days of the season." At "two minutes past 8:30 (p.m.), Tom Melville, the referee, and his assistant, Johnny Brennan, called the teams to the centre for preliminary instruction and admonition." After the meeting, the game commenced with Quebec jumping all over the Canadiens from the start, before the Canadiens, and especially their star player, Ditre "The Human Rubber Ball" Pitre, woke up and started fighting back by scoring twice. "Barney Holden (Quebec) nipped their ambition in the bud, however, by scoring for Quebec on a beautiful long side shot." The "irrepressible" Pitre retaliated by scoring again, and then another goal was quickly followed by "Newsey" Lalonde of the Canadiens.

"With the narrow margin of a one goal lead, Quebec went into the fray in the third with winning stride. The Canadiens seemed no less determined, but try as they could they were unable to penetrate the Quebec defence game. Moran, Hall, and Holden gave a great exhibition, while the forwards helped them out and

kept up an incessant attack on the Canadien goals.
Moran had not a great deal to do, but Paddy was
there with the goods when occasion demanded. The
blocking of Hall and Holden were very effective and
their rushes up the ice were features."

Malone also played a fine game until he re-injured his shoulder
and had to leave the ice. As usual, Lalonde and Pitre were the
stars for the Canadiens, as was "Rocket" Power on the defense,
who was making his first appearance for the Canadiens against
his former teammates. Holden, Oatman, and Hall of Quebec
served time in the box for tripping, as did Lalonde, Pitre and
Power for the Canadiens.

Barney finished his only season with the Quebec Bulldogs
by being hailed by sportswriters as "the best coverpoint
in the league," especially after a superb performance in a
Quebec-Wanderer match-up. The article further stated that his
outstanding play was creating quite a "furore in the National
Hockey Association." Unfortunately, the Bulldogs would finish
in last place with a 4-12 record. Jack McDonald scored 14 goals
and Tommy Dunderdale scored 13 in a 16-game season. The
next year the Bulldogs would go from last to first, winning the
Stanley Cup by defeating Victoria in 2 games, 9-3 and 8-0.
Barney probably kicked himself over his decision to move from
the Bulldogs the year before to his next team, the Saskatoon
Wholesalers. Hopefully he wasn't the type of person who dwelled
in the past! But for whatever reason, most likely monetary, he
left Quebec for Saskatchewan.

CHAPTER 6

SASKATOON WHOLESALERS ...AND BEYOND

"Barney Holden had a long and brilliant career on the ice."

- A Vancouver, B.C. newspaper article reflecting on Barney's hockey career, 1922

It is here where Barney's career data and statistics become somewhat sketchy. He moved from the Quebec Bulldogs to the Saskatoon (Saskatchewan) Wholesalers of the City Senior League (also referred to as the Saskatchewan Professional League) in 1911, where he played with future greats Hector "Hec" Fowler, and Samuel "Rusty" Crawford. Holden's stats are the only evidence that he was a member of this team. Neither the Saskatchewan Sports Hall of Fame and Museum, nor the Sports Editor for the Saskatoon Star-Phoenix, know anything about the Wholesalers. They just seemed to have vanished in the mists of time. Pity. But hard-core hockey enthusiasts know that Saskatoon had a very successful season and challenged for the Stanley Cup, failing in the attempt.

For whatever reason, Barney only played eight games with Saskatoon, but still scored six goals. Perhaps he was chosen only to fill in when needed. He played in the only games in which Saskatoon challenged for the Stanley Cup, but failed in the attempt. He led the series in penalty minutes, which prompted one hockey historian to quip, "maybe he was miffed about not scoring!" He was 31 years old at the time, and probably wondered, like all professional athletes do, how long his career might last. So for whatever reason, after the 1912 season he hung up his skates. Or so it seemed. Apparently there is evidence that he ended up playing two more seasons for the Winnipeg Victorias, but this is speculative and has been difficult to verify. Let's say for the sake are argument that he did. If so, Barney must have thought he had a little gas left in the old engine to keep going a couple more years.

Whether it was 1912, or 1914, he did eventually quit the game. His hockey income had been supplemented by working long hours in lumber mills and sash and door factories. Being a good Irish Catholic, his family continued to grow and he knew he needed more stability. So he retired from professional hockey and focused on his expanding family.

In the early 1920's a flu epidemic broke out in Raymore, Saskatchewan. Mary Holden spent much of her time tending to the sick. Barney was stricken with the flu, and became quite sick, but eventually recovered. Certainly, he must have thought about his friend and team mate, Joe Hall, who has passed away from the flu only a few years prior. Unfortunately, the illness aggravated Holden's underlying asthma condition, as well as his chronic allergy to wood dust. His health was never really the same. The fact that he was a chain-smoker all his life didn't help either.

In 1922, Barney relocated the family to Vancouver, B.C. where he took a job with the Rat Portage Lumber Company. He must have still had a little wind left in him as he managed to play baseball for the B.C. Electric team that same year. The Vancouver paper, reporting on the arrival of Barney in Vancouver, referred to him as having had a "long and brilliant career on the ice," stating he had hung up his skates in 1912, after a year with the Saskatoon Wholesalers, to devote his energies to commercial life. Still, Barney did manage to play a little hockey over the next few years in Manitoba and Saskatchewan in what were called "exhibition" leagues. These leagues were formed by former amateur and professional players who just happened to live in a particular area. They would organize leagues, or perhaps even just a few games, and challenge other teams. So while it was probably pretty good hockey, it was strictly amateur, and more or less for the pure enjoyment of the game. Barney's last recorded games were played in the Saskatoon Senior Exhibition League during the season of 1914-1915.

Barney did manage to keep in touch with a few old his old team mates. He was especially fond of Paddy Moran and Tommy Dunderdale, and he followed the remaining years of their careers as best he could. Once he relocated the family to Vancouver, B.C., Canada, he was able to talk with Fred Taylor occasionally. There is no evidence to suggest they were close friends during their playing years, but as the time flew by, and realizing they had shared so much history, they would become good friends in their golden years. "Cyc" Taylor, a competitor to the end, would outlive Holden by thirty years.

Several of Barney's contemporaries went on the play for another decade, many ending up in either the Hockey Hall of Fame, one of the provincial halls, or both. While it's a pity he did not end up in the any of the Hockey Halls of Fame, several things appeared to work against Holden.

Firstly, Barney was a defenseman, and as such didn't accumulate the scoring numbers as a forward might. That wasn't his job.

Secondly, he did not stay in the game long enough to really establish himself in the burgeoning National Hockey League.

And thirdly, he always seemed to walk in the shadow of Hod Stuart, often being compared to the greatest cover point of all time, who was tragically killed in 1907 while still in his prime. For the remainder of his professional career, Barney still walked in the footsteps of a ghost.

CHAPTER 7

ONE LAST GAME

"Can't let these kids get cocky. The old man is always right, you know."

- Barney Holden, after throwing a younger opponent over his hip in the 1933 NHL old-timer game

Thirteen of the greatest names in hockey strapped on skates and hit the ice in front of a roaring crowd in Vancouver, B.C., Canada on November 27, 1933. In the end, the old-time professionals, together worth more than a half million dollars in their prime, had too much "razzle-dazzle" left for a team of local Vancouver amateurs, and beat them 5-1, according to Hal Straight of the Vancouver Sun.

The passion in the old-timers had never abated over the years as they grabbed their sticks and coasted on the ice just one more time. There is no doubt that Barney enjoyed his return to the rink. Hearing the crowd cheer, he probably flashed the occasional smile. He felt his skate blades cutting through the ice, and most likely grinned realizing he had one last chance to knock an opponent on his keister. He no doubt stopped, looked around, and said to himself, "well, old-timer, this is it."

Even the old animosities surfaced, humorous though they were decades later.

"I shouted at that bald-headed old buzzard (Fred "Cyc" Taylor) for a pass through the season in those old days, and I've never had it yet," kidded Mickey MacKay. "You see those gray hairs?" That's because I worried about Taylor not passing the puck. He talks about his goal averages. What would he have done if I hadn't made the opening?"

After the first period, Jack Walker, Bernie Morris, and Frank Foyston sat in one corner together and moaned: "Won't that guy Taylor ever pass the puck." Even Fred Taylor, Jr. "bawled the devil out of his father" for hogging the puck. "Why don't you pass it!" he said. Fred Sr. replied that he thought he saw an opening each time. Old habits die hard, even for the old-timers.

> "Barney Holden, who displayed his best form for the old Quebec team and the Winnipeg Shamrocks when you and I weren't even thought of, Maggie, went out there with the old-time fire in his eye. It was Barney's rugged body check that swept the entire bottom shelf of Editor Billy Finlay's teeth down his throat in a game long, long ago in Winnipeg."

Holden, defending himself for throwing an opponent over his hip, exclaimed: "Can't let these kids get cocky. The old man is always right, you know." He really enjoyed that.

The old-timers who came to play that night were Clarence Boucher, Fred Taylor, Lorne Hannay, Fred McCulloch, Ernie "Moose" Johnson, Si Griffis, Mickey MacKay, Jack Walker, Frank Foyston, Bernie Morris, Frank Frederickson, Clarence (Bowdy) Boucher, Roy Rickey, and, of course, Barney Holden. Their manager was the legendary Frank Patrick. Enrie Johnson even pulled out his famous "long spliced hockey stick" that he had used with effect in the old days. The proceeds of the exhibition game went to the Santa Claus Fund for children.

> "The years have taken much of the old fire out of the limbs of the old boys, but the spirit is still there. When they left last night the most gratifying applause was the loud cry for more. And so the old-timers have come…and really showed us something. We must remember them now, for as Cyclone Taylor says: 'we'll never come back again. It was a great show.

We did all right. Nobody dropped dead. But I doubt if it will ever happen again.'"

He was right.

EPILOGUE

///////////////////////////////////////

As Barney grew older his coughing increased, especially in the evening. He spent many years working around wood dust, and most likely he was allergic to the lumber as well. A lifetime of smoking didn't help his condition.

In July 1986, Barney's grandson, Daniel Jr., exchanged letters with "Cyclone" Taylor's son, Fred, who was 67 years old at the time. Fred, Jr. recalled how, in the 1930's, his father would take him and his brother to the Saturday night games at Bob Brown's Athletic Park in Vancouver, B.C. to watch the Holden brothers playing in the Senior Baseball League. "If the Fireman were playing you could always be assured Barney would be in attendance. Son, Larry Holden, was a prominent member of the Firemen's baseball team; and Barney was always on hand to cheer the team, and hope for the big win." Fred explained that Barney and Cyclone often bumped into each other during the night games. "Dad and Barney often greeted one another warmly and after swapping a yarn or two we'd move along to our respective seats." Fred continued, "the Holden family have quite a history in sports that goes back a long way. Barney started it all and it continued from there."

In his final years Barney spent most of his time sitting in the parlour, or out on the wide verandah of his great big old wooden house in the Kitsalino area of Vancouver, B.C., Canada. His keen interest in sports never waned and he followed all of the local teams. He'd sit, sip Irish whiskey, and watch his five sons come and go from one sporting event to another. His wife, Mary, always kept a big pot of stew boiling through out the day and early evening for her hungry men.

Before he died in 1948, Barney watched all of his sons make their mark in city and regional league baseball. Three of his sons served in the Canadian armed forces during WWII. His youngest son, Danny, born when Barney was 45 years old, signed a contract with the Brooklyn Dodgers in 1944 and soon moved down to the United States. That was, perhaps, Barney's proudest moment. He tried to watch as many of his son's games as he could, but as he grew older his asthma kept him away from the baseball stadiums - too much dust. He was rarely able to attend any of his youngest son's games. Family friend, Irv Moldowan, would occasionally drop by and take Barney to Irv's semi-pro baseball games just to get the old man out of the house. All of his children were out on their own by then, including Danny who was bouncing across the U.S. for the Brooklyn Dodgers minor league organization.

After the war, in 1946, like most families, everyone came home to a major housing shortage and the big old house in "Kits" was soon bursting at the seams for a year or two. Eddie was back from the service, daughter Alice, with husband George and granddaughter, Rita, moved in for awhile. Leo and Roy also returned home, but with English brides and English toddlers in tow. They all asked to move back into Barney's house until they were back on their feet. Barney agreed, as long as the English women knew their place, and that his grandchildren were raised as good Catholics.

For Barney, it was wonderful at first, just like the old days with all of his children back home again. Every evening the neighborhood rang with the sounds of "Danny Boy," "Mother Macree," and "The Old Rugged Cross." Wife, Mary, and sons, Larry and Eddie, took turns pounding on the piano, Leo strummed his guitar and sang baritone, daughter Alice sang soprano, and whenever he was in town, Danny sang Irish tenor.

However, after all these years, Barney, the undisputed head of the household, and the crusty old Irish-Catholic, still had little love for the English, and even less for Protestants. One morning, Leo's wife, Ivy, tried to please the old man by fixing him a traditional English breakfast of sausages, eggs, etc. Unfortunately, she chose to do this on a Friday, when Catholics traditionally did not eat meat. Jesus, Mary, and Joseph! Barney flew into a rage. You'd have thought poor Ivy had just violated all Ten Commandments at once. But the party was really over when the local parish priest stopped by one day top tell Ivy and Roy's wife, Doris, that their daughters were "bastards" because they weren't married in the Catholic Church. Leo burst through the door and told the old priest just where he could put his accusation!

Eventually the three Holden brothers, and sister Alice, would move their families out from under the old man's roof. They lived in basements and attics, anywhere but under Barney's dark, intimidating Catholic regime.

As Barney grew older, to some he became a grouchy old son-of-a-gun. But others loved him in spite of his gruff demeanor. Regardless, his health was failing, and finances were tight as his children moved in and out of his home. The family tried to hang on to the memories of the early years, when Barney was healthy and full of life. He loved to dance his version of an Irish jig in the kitchen, and remove his false teeth and chase his kids around the house. But when it came to politics, religion, and sports, especially hockey, he always had an opinion and was never afraid to back it up. That never changed.

Barney's asthma continued to worsen, as did his general health. On October 27, 1948, at 8:30 p.m., as Barney lay in bed, he suddenly held up three fingers…then closed his eyes and passed away. To his family and friends keeping a bedside vigil in the dark room, the meaning of his three-fingered signal was plainly obvious. Barney, the old baseball player, was acting as his own umpire…and he had just called himself *out* after a third strike. And so with his usual shrewd sense of humor, Barney Holden, one of the very first professional hockey players in history, passed away at the age of 67. Sportswriters eulogized Barney as one of the true pioneers of early hockey, and a player whose wrist-shot was so powerful he once broke a two-inch board at the end of a rink in Brandon, Manitoba, Canada.

In the 1930's, an article appeared in the Canadian Sports and Outdoor Life magazine. It was reprinted again in the fall 1996 issue of The Icelandic Canadian Magazine. The article was about the Falcons, the 1920 Winnipeg team that won Canada's first Olympic hockey gold medal - the country's first gold medal. The article reminisced about some of the old Manitoba teams and the stars of a bygone time. Along with the original Falcons, the writer gave a tip of the hat to the other talented Winnipeg hockey players who came before the Falcons and provided the foundation for such a great team.

> "When reminiscing, the wonderful talent of Winnipeg during that era should not be overlooked. So let us digress for a moment. Never the light of day shone on finer specimens of manhood than were to be found connected with athletic clubs of Winnipeg at that time...Those were the days when 'Barney' Holden, Fred Lake and Riley Hern were the ideals of aspiring hockey players...."

Hockey Halls of Fame or not, Barney Holden had established himself as one of the early stars of professional hockey, and proved to be an inspiration to legions of players that came after.

WHAT EVER HAPPENED TO....?

EDOUARD "NEWSY" LALONDE
Born 1887, Cornwall, Ontario, Canada.
Died November 21, 1970.

Lalonde earned his nickname by working in a local newsprint plant as a youth. He excelled at his two chosen sports, lacrosse and hockey, and made his debut in organized hockey with Cornwall in 1905. This squad was known as the "Sweepers" because the players cleared the ice in lieu of renting it. An offer came from the Sault Ste. Marie franchise in the International Hockey League, the first professional circuit in North America. The team across the river in Sault Ste. Marie, Michigan tried to obtain his services, but the Canadian Soo matched the American offer and kept the young star in town. In 1907, Lalonde joined the Toronto club of the newly formed Ontario Professional Hockey League. This was where he first gained wide attention by winning the scoring race with 29 goals in only nine matches. The Toronto squad captured the inaugural OPHL crown that year but lost out to the Montreal Wanderers in the Stanley Cup challenge. In 1911-12, Lalonde headed west to play with the Vancouver Millionaires of the Pacific Coast Hockey Association, where he led the league with 27 goals. The next year he returned to the Canadiens and won another NHA scoring championship. His offensive talents were a significant factor behind the franchise's first Stanley Cup title in 1915-16. Lalonde remained with the Canadiens when the club joined the NHL in 1917-18. His scoring continued and he led all NHL scorers in 1918-19 and 1920-21. On January 19, 1920, he scored six goals in one game. He was traded to the Saskatoon Sheiks, and in his first year in Saskatchewan, player coach Lalonde added the Western Canada Hockey League scoring title to his list of accomplishments. Lalonde returned to the NHL as coach of the New York Americans in 1927. He also coached the Ottawa Senators and Montreal Canadiens before leaving the game for good in 1935. He was inducted into the Hockey Hall of Fame in 1950.

A recent on-line auction house was selling a letter written by LaLonde on February 6, 1970, while living in a nursing home in Montreal. "I am living in an old folks home," he wrote, "I lost my wife 2 years ago. This is a splendid place a 14 story bldg with 250 gentlemen and ladys (sic) all over 70 years." It is hard to imagine one of the world's best hockey and lacrosse players ended his days in a quiet nursing home. Hockey fans would have loved it if in his old age he did something marvelous like bust the cook in the chops for serving his soup cold.

JOHN L (JACK) "DOC" GIBSON
Born September 10, 1880, Ontario, Canada;
died November 1, 1954, Calgary, Alberta

In 1897, at age 17, Gibson played on a team with two famous Canadians, Edward and Joseph Seagrams, who made their mark on the world in the distilling business. Gibson went south to the United States and studied medicine in Detroit. In 1901 he set up a dental business in Houghton, Michigan. By 1902 Gibson had packed his team with old Canadian teammates, and he led the team, the Portage Lakers, through 14 consecutive win and the championship of the United States. He helped establish the International League comprised of Portage Lake, Houghton, Calumet, American Soo, Canadian Soo, and Pittsburgh. This was the very first professional hockey league in history. In 1904 Gibson and the Portage Lakers scored 273 goals, while giving up only 48. In 1905, Gibson retired from playing hockey but remained active in the league, helping to attract top Canadian talent.

JOSEPH HENRY HALL (AKA "BAD" JOE HALL)
Defense, Shoots Right, 5'10", 175 lbs. Born Staffordshire,
England, May 3, 1882, Died April 5, 1919.

Joe Hall was raised in Winnipeg and Brandon, Manitoba and was a member of teams in both cities in the Manitoba Hockey League. In 1905-06, Hall joined the Portage Lake team of the International Professional Hockey League, but stayed for only one season before returning to more familiar surroundings with Brandon. Hall had a reputation of *going after* an opposing player right from the beginning if he heard that player was out to get him. In January of 1907, Hall was added to the roster of the Kenora Thistles squad that defeated the Montreal Wanderers in a two-game Stanley Cup challenge. The next year, "Bad" Joe Hall was expelled from the Manitoba Hockey League for his rough play. The suspension was lifted quickly, but Hall finished the remainder of his hockey career in the east.

Hall was a member of the Montreal Shamrocks, a team that left the Canadian Hockey Association for the new National Hockey Association (NHA) in 1909-1910. In that same year, Hall punched referee Rod Kennedy after a fight with Renfrew's Frank Patrick. Hall was suspended and fined, and then joined the Quebec Bulldogs for the next season. As a member of Quebec, Hall was moved back to the cover-point position (defense). As a defender, Hall played a huge role in leading his Bulldogs to a Stanley Cup championship in 1912. The Quebec Bulldogs repeated as champions the following season, again with Hall anchoring the defense. With the formation of the National Hockey league, Joe Hall joined the Montreal Canadiens for its first two seasons. On January 28, 1918, Hall was engaged in a stick swinging incident with Alf Skinner of the Leafs. Both players were charged by the Toronto police with disorderly conduct and subsequently released with suspended sentences.

During the 1918-1919 Stanley Cup finals, the Spanish influenza hit many of the Montreal players during Game 5 of the series in Seattle. The flu had been brought back from Europe by the soldiers returning from WWI. It swept through North America and killed thousands of people. During the game against the Seattle Metropolitans, Joe Hall of the Canadiens, and Cully Wilson of Seattle, both fell to the ice stricken by the illness. Hall had a temperature of 105. "Bad" Joe Hall died in a hospital six days later on April 5, 1919 at the young age of 36. The Stanley Cup finals, tied at 2 games each for Montreal and Seattle was never completed. Seventeen years of professional hockey couldn't stop this guy, but a flu bug would take his life. Hall was inducted into Hockey's Hall of Fame in 1961. *Ultimate Hockey* (Toronto 1999) voted Hall the "toughest player" and "best body checker" from 1910-1919.

MAURICE JOSEPH "PHANTOM JOE" MALONE
*Center/Left Wing, Shoots Left, 5'10", 150 lbs. Born Quebec
City, Quebec, February 28, 1890, Died May 15, 1969.*

Joe Malone is best known as the NHL's first scoring leader as
he tallied up 48 points (44-4-48) in the NHL's inaugural season
of 1917-18. Malone also led the league in scoring in the 1919-
20 season with 39 goals and 10 assists winning the Ross Trophy.
He was a dangerous goal scorer, on par with Newsy Lalonde,
another gifted goal scorer from his era. The "phantom" was a
magician with the stick and respected for his fair play. Malone
was a star player long before the formation of the NHL. As a
member of the NHA he once scored 44 goals in 22 games for
a 2.2 average. Even Wayne Gretzky couldn't beat that record.
Malone also led the NHA in scoring twice. Malone was inducted
into Hockey's Hall of Fame in 1950.

SPRAGUE HORACE "PEG" CLEGHORN
Born: *March 11, 1890* **Died:** *June 20, 1956*

In 1924, when he was with the Montreal Canadiens, Cleghorn
was driving enroute to a Stanley Cup party at the home of
their coach, Leo Dandurand, when he stopped to fix a flat tire.
Unloading the truck to fetch the spare, he set the prized cup on
the side of the road so he could keep an eye on it. In a rush,
Sprague hurriedly fixed the tire, and then drove off, not wanting
to be late for the party. When he arrived at Dandurand's home
for the celebration, all of the Canadian players approached him
asking to hold the cup once more. Cleghorn paused for a second,
and then a feeling of terror overwhelmed him as he realized he
had left the cup on the side of the road! In a panic, he ran to
his car and tore down the road kicking up dust and rocks for
the entire two hours until he arrived at the place where he had
changed his tire. To his surprise, there was the cup, on the side
of the road, right where he left it. Whew!

Sprague Cleghorn was known as one of the roughest and dirtiest players of all time. One night, Cleghorn was skating down the ice, and "King" Clancey of the Maple Leafs was skating towards Sprague and called for a pass. Cleghorn, without looking, assumed the call came from a teammate and passed the puck to Clancey who proceeded to score against Cleghorn's team. After the game, King was marveling at how he had outsmarted Cleghorn. Then he heard someone say, "you forgot something on the ice, King" and when he turned around Sprague slugged him and knocked him out. When asked about this after the game, Sprague said,

"I just went over there to pat him on the head, and say what a good game he played." Cleghorn died on June 20, 1956, of injuries received two weeks earlier after being hit by a car.

JAMES OGILVIE "ODIE" CLEGHORN
Born: *September 19, 1891* **Died:** *July 13, 1956*

Odie Cleghorn was found dead in his bed just hours before his brother Sprague's funeral on July 13, 1956. Odie and Sprague were very close, "'like twins" according to Canadiens coach Leo Dandurand. The stress of the loss of his brother likely contributed to his heart failure.

EDGAR ERNEST "ED" DEY
Born: *April 30, 1884* **Died:** *February 12, 1912*

Edgar Dey, who played for the NHA Haileybury team of 1911, was featured on some of the earliest trading cards. He died as the result of an altercation in a game in Halifax. It seems he was struck on the head, and after a couple of days decided to check into hospital. It was too late; he died on February 12, 1912.

"GOLDIE" COCHRANE
Born: 1882 Died: ?

Goldie Cochrane was born in Berlin (later renamed Kitchener), Ontario in 1882. His hockey career started in Berlin in the 1890s. In 1900 he joined the Berlin Senior team and later the Senior team in Galt. He was soon recognized as one of the game's finest players. In 1907 he left the area to play for Houghton in the IHL in Northern Michigan. His hockey career ended when he joined the Canadian Army in 1914. He was wounded overseas and returned to Canada in 1918. He located in Exeter, Ontario where for several years he coached teams in the Ontario Hockey Association. He is in the Waterloo County Hall of Fame in Ontario, Canada.

THOMAS "TOMMY" DUNDERDALE
Born: *May 06, 1887* **Died:** *December 16, 1960*

Thomas Dunderdale was the first Australian-born player to be inducted into the Hockey Hall of Fame. He was born May 6, 1887 at Bennella, Australia. His parents, who had earlier moved from England, came to Canada and settled in Ottawa, in 1904, moving on to Winnipeg nine years later. When the National Hockey Association formed in 1910, Dunderdale returned east to play with Montreal, then in 1911 with the Quebec Bulldogs. Lured to Victoria in 1912, Dunderdale remained in the Pacific Coast league through 1923, and wrapped up his playing career in 1924 with Saskatoon and Edmonton of the Western Canadian league.

While in the PCHA, he played four years with Victoria, three with Portland, then returned for five more with Victoria. Dunderdale played both centre and rover and in both 1913 and 1914 led the league in scoring. During his 12 seasons in the PCHA he scored more goals then any other player in the league, scoring in every one of Victoria's 15 games in 1914, and being named the league's all-star centre. His career total is 225 goals in 290 games, plus six goals in 12 playoff games.

Dunderdale stood only 5-foot-8 and weighed 148 pounds at the peak of his playing career. He was noted as a clever stick-handler and fast skater. When he finished playing, Dunderdale coached and managed teams in Los Angeles, Edmonton and Winnipeg and was residing in Winnipeg at the time of his death, Dec. 16, 1960.

EDWARD COLE "EDDIE" OATMAN
Born: *June 10, 1889* **Died:** *November 05, 1973*

Eddie was born in 1889 in Springford, Oxford County, Ontario. Although he never played in the National Hockey League, he was among the top goal scorers of his era. During his 32 years (1907-39) playing professional hockey, Eddie was picked 10 straight years as an all-star with the Pacific Coast Hockey Association (PCHA). He was a star with the Quebec Bulldogs when it won the 1912 Stanley Cup. Eddie played with clubs that won five league championships, and he was a successful coach and captain of five different hockey teams. He was also the subject of a Ripley's "Believe It Or Not" article for playing 32 years in professional hockey. If that wasn't enough, he also served in both World Wars. Eddie died in 1973 at the age of 74.

PATRICK JOSEPH "PADDY" MORAN
Goalie, 5'11", 180 lbs. Born: Quebec City, Quebec,
March 11, 1887, Died: 1966.

Paddy Moran was an awesome hockey player whose long career ended just a year before the formation of the National Hockey League in 1917. Moran is best remembered for his excellent goaltending which led his Quebec Bulldogs to the Stanley Cup championship in both 1912 and 1913. Moran played junior hockey in his native Quebec City with the Quebec Dominions and the Crescents on the intermediate level. His

Quebec teams, however, tended to lose more games than they won so Moran would attempt to keep the puck out of the net in any way possible. Moran played in the days prior to a goal crease being painted in front of the net and guarded his area like a stray dog with a bone. His quick stick was used for more than just deflecting shots and opposition players soon developed a healthy respect for Paddy's self-created "crease."

He was a clutch goalie and in the big games was hard to beat. His Crescents were the Canadian champions in the 1900-1901 season. Moran also minded net for the All-Montreal and Haileybury squads during the 1909-1910 campaign. Paddy Moran is now immortalized in Hockey's Hall of Fame, having been inducted in 1958.

DIDIER "OLD FOLKS" PITRE
(ALSO KNOWN AS "CANNONBALL")
Right Wing/Defense, Shoots Right, 5'11", 200 lbs. Born: Valleyfield, Quebec, September 01, 1883. Died July 29, 1934.

Didier Pitre wasn't much of a team player, but he was certainly an asset to every team in which he played. During the 1914-15 season, Pitre scored 30 goals, almost half of his Montreal Canadiens' total output for the year. It was said he had legs like "tree-trunks" and supported 200 pounds of muscle which he used as often as possible. He was a skilled skater and could shoot the puck as fast as anyone who had ever played the sport. Although best known for his time spent with the Montreal Canadiens, Pitre began playing hockey in 1903 as a member of the Montreal Nationals (who hardly won a game that year).

Beginning in 1904-1905, Pitre played three seasons with the IHL's Michigan Soo Indians and then spent time with the Montreal Shamrocks, Edmonton Eskimos and Renfrew Creamery Kings before joining the 1909 Habs squad. The defenseman/rover was moved to right wing for the 1914-15 campaign and scored an astonishing 30 goals, just 8 less than the rest of his team scored that season. In 1916, Pitre led the Montreal Canadiens to its first Cup win.

Pitre liked to hold out for more money and once signed a contract for $3,000 which was $2,500 more than the average salary at the time. In 1914, chicken wire was installed in the Victorias' arena to protect fans from his powerful shots.

FREDERICK WELLINGTON "CYCLONE" TAYLOR
Rover, Shoots Left, 5'8",165 lbs. Born: Tara, Ontario - June 23, 1884. Died June 10, 1979.

Fred Taylor was the greatest star of his era. His nicknames, "The Listowel Pistol" and his more famous "Cyclone," are tributes to his unmatched speed on the ice. He was responsible for helping bring both Ottawa and Vancouver the Stanley Cup championships. Taylor grew up in Listowel, Ontario and was banned from the Ontario Hockey Association when he refused to leave his Listowel club for the Toronto Marlboros.

Subsequently, Taylor left Ontario for Portage la Prairie, Manitoba in 1905 to play hockey. Less than a year later, Taylor signed a contract with the IHL and became a star as a member of the Houghton Portage Lakers based in Michigan. In 1907-1908, Taylor jumped to the Ottawa Senators of the ECAHA due to the failure of the IHL. When Taylor was signed by the Renfrew Creamery Kings in 1909 he reportedly signed a contract to pay him $5,250 for the 12-game season, the richest contract in North American sports history at the time (on a per-game basis). Taylor, truly one of the game's greats, earned the remarkable distinction of being named to the First All-Star Team everywhere he played from 1900 to 1918. He was inducted into Hockey's Hall of Fame in 1947.

Former teammates have accused Taylor of being a puck-hog. Interestingly enough, his biggest defender was Barney Holden's wife, Mary. She said Taylor wasn't a puck-hog, "it's just that no one could keep up with him."

SILAS SETH "SI" GRIFFIS

Born September 22, 1883, Onaga, Kansas. Died July 9, 1950.

Griffis was a very fast skater despite his large frame. His speed enabled him to dominate as a rover and defender. He contributed to the Kenora Thistles' Stanley Cup triumph in 1907 and later captained the Vancouver Millionaires to the Stanley Cup in 1915. Griffis joined the Rat Portage club in the newly formed Manitoba and Northwest Hockey League in 1902. His play as a rover and cover point contributed significantly to the team's 1902-03 league title. The circuit was reorganized into the Manitoba Senior Hockey League in 1905.

By 1907, the Rat Portage club had been renamed the Kenora Thistles and was even more talented than before. They captured the Stanley Cup in a thrilling two-game series with the Montreal Wanderers in January 1907. Griffis debuted on the West Coast by scoring twice and adding two assists in his new club's opener on January 5, 1912. Griffis proceeded to score 38 goals for Vancouver before retiring in 1919. He was a member of the 1915 Stanley Cup-winning Millionaires. Griffis is a member of the Northwestern Ontario Sports Hall of Fame and was elected to the Hockey Hall of Fame in 1950.

WILLIAM MILTON "RILEY" HERN

Goalie, 5'9", 170 lbs. Born: St. Mary's, Ontario,
December 05, 1880. Died: June 24, 1929.

In 1962, the Hockey Hall of Fame inducted a goaltender with career regular season totals of just 5 shutouts and a 4.33 goals against average. In fact, this goalie only appeared in 130 regular season contests!

Little is known about Hern before 1900, but from 1890s through 1911, he was able to distinguish himself as a premiere goaltender in many different levels of hockey. Hern played junior hockey in the Ontario Hockey Association on a team based in his hometown of St. Mary's. As Hern progressed through the junior and senior ranks, his goaltending led him to play for a team based in London, Ontario. Hern played the 1901-02 season as a member of the Pittsburgh Keystones in the Western Pennsylvania Hockey League. That season, Hern won 9 of the 14 games he played, leading the league in that category.

In the 1903-04 season Hern signed on with the Portage Lakers, a Michigan-based squad that played in the International Hockey League. While the records of this season are sketchy, best estimates place Hern in 16 games that year of which he won all but one. During the 1904-05 season, Hern played exceptionally well as he led the league with 2 shutouts and topped all IHL goaltenders with a 3.54 goals against average. In 24 contests, Hern scored 15 wins against 7 losses and 2 ties. Hern dominated the IHL the following season winning 15 of 20 contests while posting a shutout and 3.46 goals against average.

The following four seasons were the most successful of his career. Hern led his new team, the Montreal Wanderers to four consecutive Stanley Cup championships. The Wanderers, playing in the Eastern Canada Amateur Hockey Association, scored a perfect 10 wins in 10 games with Hern in the net during the 1906-07 campaign. Hern won three games during the Cup round to help secure the first of the four championships.

In the 1907-08 season, Hern posted an 8-2-0 record, good enough to lead all goaltenders in wins. In the Cup round, Hern was a perfect five for five with a 3.20 goals against average. After winning a third straight cup in the 1908-09 season, Hern won 11 of 12 games and won his only Cup game in the 1909-10 campaign to lead his squad to Cup number four. After a comparatively poor 1910-11 season, Riley Hern, who had his own personal business woes, retired from professional hockey, but stayed in the game as a goal judge and referee.

WILLIAM HODGESON "HOD" STUART
Point, 6'0", 190 lbs., Born Ottawa, Ontario in 1879.
Died June 23, 1907.

Stuart was known as one of the best defensemen/rovers in hockey during the first decade of the twentieth century. Some even considered Stuart the best player in the world. He played with his brother, Bruce, for the Ottawa Silver Seven and the Quebec Bulldogs of the Canadian Amateur Hockey League. Stuart had a knack for piling up penalty minutes. No one in the 1903-04 season spent more time penalized then Stuart.

He joined the Caumet Miners of the International Hockey League in 1904 and scored an impressive 18 goals in just 22 games while totaling 19 penalty minutes. Stuart played just one game with the Miners during the 1905-06 season, playing chiefly for the Pittsburgh Pros, a team with which he accumulated his greatest season total for penalty minutes with 50 in just 20 games. In the 1906-07 season, Stuart played in four contests for the Pittsburgh Pros, but he is best known for the 12 games he skated in with the Montreal Wanderers.

By the close of the 1906-07 season, Stuart was upset with the style of play in the International League. He was tired of being the target of opposing players of lesser talent whose main goal was to either cripple him, or goat him into more penalty minutes.

Hod Stuart's life ended suddenly on June 23, 1907 when he and his buddies went swimming in the Bay of Quinte, just a stone's throw from Belleville, Ontario. Stuart dived head-first into the water, unaware that there was a rock beneath the spot where he was diving. Stuart's head hit the rock and the great defenseman died almost instantly. He was only 28 years old.

Hod Stuart never played in the NHL, but was one of the twelve original inductees into the Hockey Hall of Fame in 1945. An estimated 3,800 spectators attended a "Hod Stuart Memorial Game" on January 2, 1908. The proceeds of the game went to Stuart's widow and two children, and 3,800 spectators contributed more than $2,000. It was the first such "all-star" contest in hockey.

FRED EDGAR LAKE
Born: *1882, Saskatchewan;* **Died:** *November 30, 1937*

Lake was a member of the Portage Lake team of the IHL and then joined the Ottawa Senators Hockey Club where he remained for 1909, 1910 and 1911. The Senators won the Stanley cup in 1909 and 1911. It was said he skated "like an egg-beater." After he retired from hockey he became a prominent businessman.

He died under suspicious circumstances on November 30, 1937 when his body was found in an automobile, on a deserted farm, near the Connaught Park Jockey Club in Aylmer, Quebec. An "extension" had been placed on the exhaust pipe and twisted into the interior of the car. Lake's head was resting on two small pillows, his body stretched out on the seat. It appeared to be a suicide, except for the fact that two sets of footsteps were discovered in the frozen snow leading away from the car. An "auto crank" was also found on the ground near the back wheels. The mystery behind his death was never solved.

GEORGE "SKINNER" POULIN ("THE TABASCO KID" OR JUST "KID.")
Born 1887 in Smith Falls, Ontario. Died 1971.

"The Kid" played forward for the Winnipeg Maple Leafs from 1907 to 1908, and then joined the Canadians in 1910. The Montreal Canadiens Hockey Club was established on December 4, 1909 to promote a French flavor to hockey in the Montreal area, which up to that time was predominately run by the English with clubs like the Shamrocks, Wanderers, and Victorias. The first players chosen for the new club were Edouard "Newsy" Lalonde, Didier Pitre, Art Bernies and George "Skinner" Poulin. The team earned the nickname "Habs" from the French term "les

Habitants" used to describe the hearty settlers in New France, the predecessor of what is now Quebec. The word "Canadiens" also had a similar meaning and was used to describe the local people of Montreal. Poulin was on the Canadiens team in 1913 when they defeated the Portland (Oregon) Rosebuds on March 30, 1916 to claim the Stanley Cup.

Then he seems to have disappeared.

LESTER "THE SILVER FOX" PATRICK
Born December 30, 1883, Drummondville, Quebec. Died June 1, 1960. Played 18 professional seasons from 1903 to 1926.

Beginning in 1903, Patrick played a significant role in hockey history for nearly half a century. As a player, he was one of the top rushing defensemen of his day and a team leader. Along with his brother Frank, he pioneered the construction of artificial rinks and formed the Pacific Coast Hockey Association. He learned the game in the amateur leagues of Montreal but first gained fame as a star offensive *blueliner* with Brandon, Manitoba, of the North West Hockey League. He was a key member of the squad when it issued an unsuccessful challenge for the Stanley Cup against the Ottawa Senators in March 1904.

He returned to Montreal to play a year with the Westmount club before joining the powerful Montreal Wanderers in 1905-06. He moved to Nelson, British Columbia, in 1907 to work in the family lumber business but continued to play on a local team.

Patrick returned to the headlines with the Edmonton squad that lost a Stanley Cup challenge to the Wanderers in 1908. His brother Frank joined him at this time. The Patrick brothers played with the Renfrew Millionaires during the inaugural season of the National Hockey Association in 1910-11. The following season, they returned to British Columbia and began plans for a new league of their own.

Formed in 1911-12, the Pacific Coast Hockey Association attained a reputation on par with the NHA - and later the NHL

- until it was renamed the Western Canada Hockey League. The Patricks lured away many top stars of the NHA to give their new league instant legitimacy. After leaving the NHL, Patrick took over the operation of the Victoria Cougars, a minor professional outfit in the Pacific Coast/Western Hockey League. He left that post for retirement in 1954. Patrick was elected to the Hockey Hall of Fame in 1947.

ERNIE "MOOSE" JOHNSON
Born February 26, 1886, Montreal, Quebec.
Died March 25, 1963.

"Moose" Johnson began his organized hockey career in the Montreal City League and at one time played with the junior team on a Friday night, the intermediate team the next afternoon, and the senior team on the Saturday night. He signed on with the Montreal Wanderers for the Eastern Canada Amateur Hockey Association's inaugural season of 1905-06 where he finished tenth in scoring with 12 goals in a ten-game schedule.

In March 1906 the Wanderers ended the three-year reign of the legendary Silver Seven by defeating Ottawa in a two-game challenge for the Stanley Cup. Prior to the start of the 1906-07 season the ECAHA ruled that professionals would be allowed to play with the amateurs in the league and the Wanderers were quick to sign Johnson. He eventually moved west to play for the New Westminster Royals of the Pacific Coast Hockey Association. He was a perennial all-star in the western league, making the PCHA First All-Star Team in 1912, 1913, 1915, 1916, 1917, 1918, 1919, and 1921.

It was while playing in Victoria as a member of the Cougars that he was first called *Moose*. He was noted for using the longest stick in hockey and had a 99-inch reach. His final year in the PCHA was with Victoria in 1921-22. Johnson played out his career in the minor leagues, making stops in Los Angeles, Minneapolis, Portland (Oregon), Hollywood, and San Francisco before retiring in 1931. Moose Johnson was inducted into the Hockey Hall of Fame in 1952.

ERNEST "ERNIE" RUSSELL ("INDIAN RUBBER MAN")
Born October 21, 1883 in Montreal, Quebec.
Died February 23, 1963.

Ernie Russell was a fast skater and an accomplished stick-handler, and although he weighed only about 140 pounds he averaged nearly two goals per game over his career. Russell, a pure goal scorer, twice scored 8 goals in a game, scored 6 goals in a game three times, and had four 5 goal games.

In the 1906-07 season, Russell cemented his place among hockey's elite when he racked up an astounding 42 goals in only 9 games and then scored 12 more times in five postseason games, leading his Montreal Wanderers to the Stanley Cup Championship.

In 1907, Russell scored a hat trick in five consecutive games and had goal scoring streaks of up to 10 games. That 1907 season proved to be a good year off the ice for Russell as well. He played halfback with the Montreal AAA that year when they won the Dominion Rugby Championship of Canada. He was one of Montreal's best known and most respected athletes in his day, and lived in the city his entire life. In 1965, Ernie Russell was immortalized in Hockey's Hall of Fame.

FRANK CHARLES "ONE-EYED" MCGEE
Died September 16, 1916

"One-eyed" Frank McGee, a Canadian, earned his nickname from the loss of sight in one eye in a hockey game. Nevertheless, he became a star with the Ottawa Silver Seven and set a still-standing record of 14 goals in one 1905 Stanley Cup game. He was the nephew of an assassinated Father of Canadian Confederation, Thomas D'Arcy McGee, an Irish rebel who was forced to flee to the U.S., and later moved to Montreal. Frank McGee was the very first superstar in the very first dynasty in the history of hockey. He began his hockey career with the old Aberdeens and graduated to senior hockey when he joined the Ottawa squad in 1904, remaining a member of the team until 1907. While playing with Aberdeens at Hawkesbury one night he suffered the loss of the sight of an eye when struck by a flying puck. However, the injury never impaired his game.

Though famous as a hockey player, he was also a noted football player, having played on the Ottawa City half-back line in 1897-8 when they won the Dominion championship that year.

He would somehow manage to pass the medical examination when he enlisted for service in WWI. It is said that on the eye test, he tricked the physician by first holding one hand over his bad eye to read the chart and then switching hands, instead of eyes, for the second part of the test. He was wounded in December 1915 and spent nine months in an English hospital. After he recovered, he requested that he been returned to the front as a motorcycle dispatch rider. Lieutenant McGee was killed on September 16, 1916 at Courcelitte (France) when struck by a German bullet. He died in Flanders Field. Frank was the only Hall of Fame athlete of any sport to be killed in action fighting for his country.

LITTLE IS KNOWN ABOUT THE FOLLOWING FELLOWS EXCEPT THEIR PLAYING HISTORY

Harry Bright
1901-03 Montreal Shamrocks (CAHL)
1903-05 Brandon
1904-05 Portage-La-Prairie
1905-07 Portage Lakes (IHL)
1908-09 Nelson, B.C.

Walter A. Forrest
1903-05 Berlin (WOHA)
1905-06 Portage Lakes (IHL)

William "Coonie" Shields
1901-03 Pittsburgh PAC (Senior League)
1902-03 Pittsburgh Bankers (Senior League),
1903-04 Portage Lakes (Pro XG)
1904-05 Portage Lakes (IHL)
1905-07 Calumet Wanderers (IHL)
1907-08 Referee Portage Lakes
1909-10 Moosomin (Sask, SR.).

J. E. "Grindy" Forrester
1897-99 Waterloo (Int. OHA)
1900-02 Waterloo (Sr. WOHA)
1902-04 Barrie (Sr.OHA)
1904-05 Thessalon (Int. OHA)
1905-07 Portage Lakes (IHL)
1907-08 Winnipeg Maple Leafs (MnPHL) / Pittsburgh PAC
(WPHL)
1908-09 Winnipeg Maple Leafs (MnPHL) / Weyburn
(SPHL)
1909-10 Montreal Shamrocks (IHL).

Ernie Westcott
1901-02 Pittsburgh Keystones (Senior League)
1902-05 Portage Lakes (Pro XG/IHL). (Portage Lakes Won
U.S. Professional championship in 1902-03 and 1903-04).

Bert Morrison
1897-00 Upper Canada College
1900-01 Toronto Wellingtons
1901-02 Pittsburgh Keystones (Sr.WPHL)
1902-03 North York Athletic Club

1903-05 Portage Lakes (IHL)
1905-06 Toronto Pros (Pro XG)
1906-07 Calumet Wanderers (IHL)
1907-08 Montreal Shamrocks   (ECHA)
1908-09 Toronto Pros (OPHL)
1910-11 Haileybury (TPHL)
1911-12 Toronto Tecumsehs (PRO XG).

Tom "Nibs" Phillips
1901-02 Montreal Shamrocks (Senior League)
1902-03 Montreal AAA and McGill University
1903-04 Toronto Marlboros (Senior League)
1904-05 Rat Portage Thistles (Manitoba Senior Hockey League)
1905-07 Kenora Thistles (McPHL)
1907-08 Ottawa Senators (ECHA)
1908-09 Edmonton Pros (Stanley Cup attempt)
1909-10 Nelson, 1911-12 Vancouver Millionaires (PCHA)
1913-14 Hamilton (Int. OHA) Coach
1914-16 Referee PCHA.

"Nibs" salary was $1,800 when he played for the Ottawa Senators during the 1907-08 season. It was the most paid to any player for one season, until Lester Patrick received $3,000 to play at Renfrew.

Rockett Power
1901-02 Quebec 2nds (Int.)
1902-04 Quebec (Senior League)
1903-04 Canadian Soo (Pro XG)
1904-05 Quebec (Senior League)
1907-08 Quebec (ECHA)
1908-09 Edmonton (Pro XG),
1909-10 Waterloo (OPHL)
1910-11 Montreal Canadiens (NHA)
1911-12 New Glasgow Cubs (Maritime Pro.)
1912-13 Quebec Bulldogs (NHA).

William (Billy) "Cotton-Top" Keane
A relative of Mike Keane who currently plays for the Colorado Avalanche of the NHL.
1902-05 Winnipeg Victorias (MnSHL)
1905-07 Winnipegs (MnSHL)
1907-09 Winnipeg Maple Leafs (MnPHL)
1908-09 Weyburn (SPHL).

George "Doe" Smith
1899-03 Montreal AAA (Senior League)
1903-06 Brandon (Senior League)
1906-07 Brandon Wheat Cities (MnPHL)
1908-09 Fernie, B.C. Brandon Shamrocks (SP).

Walt Bellamy
1906-07 Brandon (Manitoba Professional League)
1907-08 Strathcona (Alberta Professional League)
1908-09 Winnipeg Shamrocks (Manitoba Professional League)
/ Fort William Wanderers (Pro New Ontario League)
1909-10 Montreal Shamrocks (NHA)
1912-13 (Tryout) Toronto Tecumsehs (NHA).

HOCKEY CARD COLLECTING

Card collectors and hockey enthusiasts have accepted the "C56" set issued by Imperial Tobacco as the first hockey card set. Printed in full color in 1910-1911, the 36-card set features a host of hall-of-famers, early stars, and several legends of the game. Although referred to as "Imperial Tobacco" issues, there is no actual proof that Imperial Tobacco had anything to do with producing the set. But for some reason the name stuck.

The cards in this classic set each measure 1.5 by 2.625 inches, noticeably smaller than today's standard card size. At the bottom of the card is the player's name and team, and the card number is in the upper left-hand corner. Just inside a white border. The back of the card features crossed hockey sticks, a puck, and the words "Hockey Series" printed beneath the crossed sticks. In addition, the back also shows the player's name and team.

Since this was the very first set of hockey cards ever produced, it is highly sought after by collectors. Similar to the T-36 baseball cards, but much more affordable, these cards can still be found through card dealers. There are four key cards in the C56 set: two Art Ross rookie cards (#8, #9), Cyclone Taylor (#15), and Newsey Lalonde (#36), which can fetch up to $1,000 in mint condition. Common cards, like the Barney Holden (#4) card can be found for $350-$10,000 depending on the condition. A complete set in "excellent-mint" condition" would set you back up to $20,000. As these cards are now 93 years old, it is quite difficult to find mint condition cards. Many collectors are just happy to be able to complete the set regardless of the condition. So collectors grab what they can, often holding out hope that a card in better condition will come along.

In 1911-1912, Imperial Tobacco (again, this is speculation) issued a second set of hockey cards called "C55." These 45-card set measured the same as the C56 set and featured a similar design. The front of the card is a color portrait of the player surrounded by two hockey sticks. The back shows the words "Hockey Players" on top, followed by the player's name and the teams he has played for. As in the C56 set, each card has a number that is found in a small circle on the back. Although the C55 cards are more common than the C56 cards, there are a few very valuable cards that will prohibit the average collector from completing the set. For example, Georges Vezina (#38) is valued at $5,000 in Excellent-Mint condition, and $2,500 in Very Good-Excellent condition. Cyclone Taylor (#20), Art Ross (#31), and Newsy Lalonde (#42), Joe Malone (#4), and Paddy Moran (#1) will run you about $1,200 in Excellent-Mint condition and $600 in Very Good-Excellent condition. Common cards will cost about $60-$125 depending on the condition. The entire set will set you back about $13,000-$15,000 in Excellent-Mint condition, or about half that for Very Good-Excellent condition.

The final set issued by Imperial Tobacco in 1912-1913 was named "C57." It differs from the two previous sets in that the cards were printed in black and white, which some collectors felt added a classier old-time hockey feel. The measurements were the same as the prior two sets, and the C57 cards were very similar to the C56 set. This 50-card set is valued around $18,000 in Excellent-Mint condition and $9,999 in Very Good-Excellent condition. As with the prior sets, the cards were usually wrapped in numerical order with a rubber-band, thus damaging the first and last cards of the set. To find them in Excellent-Mint condition (especially the #1 card) increases the value, even if the player wasn't necessarily a superstar. There was no C57 Barney Holden card.

Set Name	Card #	Description	Low Price	High Price
1910-11 C56	4	B. Holden	0	$300-$10,000
1910-11 Sweet Corporal Postcards	3	B. Holden	0	$300-$10,000
1911-12 C55	3	B. Holden	0	$300-$10,000
1912-13 C57	N/A	N/A	N/A	N/A

Although the author has not checked the accuracy of the careers listed on the back of each individual card, the teams listed (and years played) on the back of Barney's cards are slightly inaccurate and/or contradictory. Even Fred Taylor's 1910 card totally omits his having played on the Portage Lake team, so it is safe to assume many of the player's cards are inaccurate as well. Barney's 1910-1911 card did place him on the Portage Lake team from 1905 to 1907. He is then listed on the Winnipeg Maple Leafs from 1908 to 1909, which is accurate, as is the claim he was on the Quebec Bulldogs in 1910. Holden's 1911-1912 card is way off-base, claiming he was on the Calumet team in 1905, and then on the Sault Ste. Marie team in 1906. This is certainly not true as he played for Portage Lake during those years. 1908 shows him on the Montreal Shamrocks, which is not true, but the claim that he was on the Winnipeg Maple Leafs in 1909 is accurate. Finally, he is listed as being on the Quebec Bulldogs in 1910 and 1911, which is not true. By 1911, Barney had moved on to the Saskatoon Wholesalers and the team was challenging for the Stanley Cup. Makes you wonder who researched these cards anyway?

Thanks to Keith Lenn @ hockeysandwich.com and Beckett.com

BARNEY HOLDEN
INDIVIDUAL CAREER STATISTICS
(Courtesy of LostHockey.com)

Year	Team	League	GP	G	A	Pts	PIM
1902-03	Winnipeg Shamrocks	Man NW	5	5	?	5	?
1904-05	Portage Lakes	IHL	24	9	0	9	47
1905-06	Portage Lakes	IHL	20	9	0	9	31
1906-07	Winnipeg Strathconas	ManPro	1	1	0	1	0
	Portage Lakes	IHL	20	4	3	7	35
1907-08	Winnipeg Maple Leafs	ManPro	15	4	0	4	0
	Winnipeg Maple Leafs	Stanley Cup	2	0	0	0	2
1908-09	Winnipeg Maple Leafs	ManPro	4	1	2	3	6
	Winnipeg Maple Leafs	Stanley Cup	5	2	2	4	3
1909-10	Montreal Shamrocks	CHA	3	1	0	1	0
	Montreal Shamrocks	NHA	12	0	5	5	23
1910-11	Quebec Bulldogs	NHA	16	4	0	4	40
1911-12	Saskatoon Wholesalers	Ssk-Pro	7	6	0	6	0
		Stanley Cup	1	0	0	0	12*
1912-13	Winnipeg Victorias	XG?	*Statistics Unavailable*				
1913-14	Winnipeg Victorias?	XG?	*Statistics Unavailable*				
1914-15	Saskatoon Senior	X G	*Statistics Unavailable*				

* Led the series in penalty minutes

Key to Statistics

GP	– Games played
G	– Goals
A	– Assists
Pts or TP	– Total Points
(+/-)	– Plus / Minus
PIM	– Penalty Minutes
PP	– Power Play Goals
SH	– Shorthanded Goals
GW	– Game Winning Goals
GT	– Game-tying Goals
SOG	– Shots on Goal
MIN	– Total Minutes Played
GA	– Goals Against
GAA	– Goals Against Average
SV	– Saves
SA	– Shots Against
S% or SPCT	– Save Percentage
SO	– Shutouts

ABOUT THE AUTHOR

Dan Holden, Jr. was born in Eugene, Oregon in 1958, the son of a former Brooklyn Dodger minor leaguer, and the grandson of Barney Holden,. He majored in Journalism at Oregon State University where he wrote for a number of college publications... and played a little rugby.

He currently writes articles that focus primarily on Irish history, sports history, and the American Civil War. His articles appeared monthly in the *Irish American* newspaper in Philadelphia, PA under the byline, *Holden's Historical Review.* His history articles have also been featured in *The Celtic Chronicles* (Pacific Northwest), *The Irish Times Magazine* (San Francisco), *The Irish Eye* (Upper Delaware Valley), and *Military History* magazine.

Holden's first book was entitled, *Ireland: Too Long a Sacrifice,* and was nominated for the 2003 Oregon Book Awards. He is currently working on a book about semi-pro baseball in Vancouver, B.C., Canada from 1920-1960.

His most recent works included a story about his father entitled, *Root for the Irish Kid!* that appeared in *The Oregonian* (Portland, Oregon) in June 2004, and was selected from numerous entries to appear in the "My Turn" section of *The Eugene Register-Guard* (Eugene, Oregon) for the Father's Day issue.

Holden also wrote a two-part article about his return to the rugby pitch at the age of 45 entitled, *The Ruck, the Maul and the Joy of Surviving it all*, and, *It Seemed Like a Good Idea at the Time.* Both of these articles appeared in *Rugby Magazine* (New York) in February and June 2004.

He has been married to Barbara for 19 years and is the father of two daughters.

BIBLIOGRAPHY

- **A Brief History of Hurling,** Lady Elisabetta Maidestro
- **AZHockey.com**
- **Birthplaceofhockey.com**
- **Canadian SPORTS Collector,** May 2001 *(www.CSCMAG.ca)*
- **Colin Nickerson**, "The Irish Flourish Among the French in Quebec," Boston Globe, 2000.
- **Cyclone Taylor**, "A Hockey Legend," Eric Whitehead, Toronto, 1977."
- **Did Waterford Hurlers Invent the Game of Ice-Hockey?** John O'Connor, Munster Express, July 26, 2002
- **ePenaltyBox.com**
- **From Prairie Wool to Golden Grain: Raymore Sask. and District, 1904-1979**
- **Hockey Hall of Fame**
- **Hooked on Hockey**, Alan Ross, Walnut Grove Press, 1999
- **Houghton Daily Mining Gazette** (1904-1907)
- **International Fire Fighter,** October 1932
- **Hockey Through The Early Years of Raymore, Sask,** Alne Cameron
- **Longhorn Ice Hockey**, 2001
- **Losthockey.com**
- **Legendsofhockey.net**
- **Montreal Gazette** (1908)
- **National Library of Canada** (*www.nlc.bnc.ca*)
- **Northern Gaels Hurling Club,** Finland
- **Okanagan Commoner**, September 3, 1925
- **Ottawa Free Press** (1908)
- **Stanley Cup Fever**, Brian Mcfarlane
- **The International Hockey League and the Professionalization of Ice Hockey, 1904-1907;** Daniel S. Mason, Faculty of Physical Education and Recreation, University of Alberta

- **The Trail of the Stanley Cup,** Alan Hustak; Charles Coleman
- **The Pictorial History of Hockey**, Gallery Books Corp., New York, 1987
- **Those Were the Days: The Lore of Hockey by the Legends of the Game**"; Stan Fischler, Dodd, Mead & Co., New York, 1976
- **U.S. Hockey Hall of Fame**
- **Ultimate Hockey,** Weir, Chapman; Stoddard Publishing, Toronto, 1999
- **Vancouver Sun** (1933)
- *www.hockeysandwich.com*
- *www.ottawavalleyonline.com*
- **Winnipeg Province** (1928)
- **Winnipeg Tribune Magazine** (1933)

"I can hear the roar of the runners yet, and see the white powder fly as the leader doubled and the whole pack ground their skate blades to the ice and reversed in pursuit. I can still feel the sting of the cold December evening on my hot cheeks as I went for my coat when the game was over...The boys are at it yet, though they all have 'store sticks' and call the game *hockey.*

Walter Pritchard Eaton (1878-1957)
American author, critic, and educator;
Associate Professor of Playwriting at Yale

Outing Magazine, December 1913